The Unknown Tales

By: Lauren Anderson

To anyone who's
story feels overlooked and unknown,
may you never forget that you are a part of someone
else's and someone else a part of yours.

— Lauren

Contents

Prologue

Everyone knows tales of Cinderella, Sleeping Beauty, Snow White, and of course Beauty & The Beast.

Everybody knows their stories, but what about the characters behind the scenes? They step out only when needed, but they're the most important part. Nobody knows their stories.

Why are they how they are? How did they become who they are? Where did they get into a tale that is actually known? The stories that they appear in only once or twice, are the only parts of their lives that anybody knows about.

In this book, we will be reading deeper than the surface. We will dive into the back stories of our beloved characters, saviors, and villains...

Chapter One

Edna lived in a small village.

Her mother sold flowers and her father owned a tiny Inn on the other side of town.

Her father was very welcoming; one of the reasons he opened his own Inn. Even if someone doesn't have enough money, he would give them a discount or let them stay there free of charge.

A quote of his that he often used was, "generosity is like a boomerang, if you throw it out into the wind, it will be returned to you."

Edna didn't understand why he used metaphors for people, but it was his quote, not hers.

One morning, Edna was woken up by a loud trumpet.

She peered out her window to see what was causing the commotion. Outside she saw many of the Royal Guards from the palace. A palace that Edna saw outside her window everyday; or at least the top of the palace, through the forest stretched out between them.

Edna ran downstairs to see why all the Royal Guards were in her small village.

She gracefully galloped down the stairs, then swung into the kitchen off the oak banister.

To her surprise, her mother wasn't pruning the flowers in the vase like she always did in the mornings. Instead, she was gawking out the window.

Edna tried getting her attention by asking "mother?" But she wouldn't respond. All she did was stare out the window. Edna knew it had to do with the guards to make her mother act this way. So, she just let mother stare.

A few moments later, mother ordered in a panicked voice, "Edna, get your father from the field! NOW!"

Knowing now that something was definitely not right, Edna hurried into the field beyond their backyard.

She jumped over the rotten log where the fox lived, dodged the trees where the birds sang, then crossed the river where the fish swam.

She finally entered the field where the crops grew, and saw father picking the flowers for mothers sale that day.

Edna bolted towards him in distress.

"Father! Father!" Edna cried, "mother told me to come get you! There are soldiers in the village!"

Father shook his head, "Don't worry, Edna, they are probably just here for the taxes. I'll be back soon."

She grabbed father's arm out of nervousness. "No father! No! They were rummaging through stores and houses!"

Father's eyes widened in alarm, then he too, started to bolt.

Once we made it to the house, we saw mother crying at the table.

Father knelt down beside her, "darling, what's the matter?!"

She sniffed then answered "The king is taking whatever he believes is his!"

Mother looked deep into father's eyes, then exclaimed "Honey, I'm so sorry, but he took your Inn..."

Father's hands dropped from mother's shoulders, to his sides. Instead of being on one knee, he collapsed to two.

His Inn was his life, it was his living and calling. He worked everyday, counted every cent for thirty years!...now it is gone...

But father wiped away his tears and declared "my Inn may be gone, but my family is right here, and that is all I need."

He wrapped his arm around mother, then stuck his other arm out to Edna, but she was not as comforted.

She didn't understand what father meant. The Inn was his everything. He knew that Inn longer than he knew mother or her. He welcomed people of every background, every town, every kingdom. His guests were his family, mother and her were just there to help run it. She couldn't believe...no, she wouldn't believe father meant that.

Instead of embracing, she ran out the door. She heard father and mother's voices calling for her to come back, but she knew she couldn't allow some greedy king to wreck her father's family. She knew she had to do something, she just didn't know what yet...

She ran farther into town and finally reached the edge of the village. Before she stepped over the line, she looked back at her beautiful village.

The luscious gardens, the dazzling streams, the brick houses, and most of all, the wonderful people.

She remembered Ms. Green, who helped her draw water from the well, or Mr. Gray, who told her amazing stories of how he used to be a prince, then was chased out of the castle by wild dogs, and could never find his way back. However, Mr. Gray was later proved to be a liar who also sold a painted egg saying it was an egg that dropped from a rainbow....

She knew she would miss everybody terribly, but no King should get away with wrecking everyone's life.

She tightened her fists and charged for the forest, where her journey begins....

She was deep in the forest now. She's never seen it before, only from a long distance from her window.

Even though the forest was gorgeous, it was also terrifying.

Everything moved, everything was alive and watched you, but everything was dead silent.

You could hear the tiny creeks of the branches, or the abrupt snap of a stick. The trees enveloped everything, even the sky could only peek through the leaves.

The wind seemed to even be timed. Every five minutes a cold gust of wind would shake the whole forest.

A tsunami of leaves would cover any grass peeking out around the roots of trees.

Edna stopped against a great oak to take a break. She had nothing to eat or drink, and she was hungry and thirsty.

She decided to get up and search for water and food.

She came across a green bush full of little blue spheres.

She's never seen anything like them before, so she wondered if they were edible.

She reached over and grabbed one blue sphere. It was soft and squishy. She held it up to her nose to smell it. It had a faint scent, but it smelled delicious. So, she took a risk and popped it into her mouth.

It had a satisfying little crunch when her teeth punctured it. The juice filled her mouth, and the taste was sweet with a hint of sour.

It was surprisingly addicting. Edna couldn't stop stuffing the blue spheres in her starving mouth.

While she was eating her way through the bush, she noticed in the corner of her eye a dark figure.

She quickly spun her head in the direction, but the figure disappeared.

A shiver ran down her spine, just like the one when her mother shouted. Something was wrong... Something was happening... Somebody or something was watching her....

She stuffed her two pockets full of the blue spheres, then bolted for the palace.

She'd been sprinting for five minutes now, still not being able to shake off the feeling of being watched.

Eventually, she came by a river. It was powerful enough to make her not want to cross. When she went to the edge, the water splashed up onto her dress.

She stumbled back from the frigid water, then wondered how she was ever going to get to the other side.

She turned around to find a possible fallen tree she could use to pass, but instead she found something much better, a bridge!

She cheerfully walked over to the wooden bridge, but before she could even take one step on to it, a big monster appeared! He had green scaly skin, with horrible decaying teeth. His claws were sharpened and his eyes were yellowish red.

Edna stumbled back at the sight of this terrifying creature. She didn't know what to say or do. Her smart self was saying "run run! Run back to your safe village! This monster will eat you!" However her courageous self was saying "even though your village doesn't have these creatures, doesn't mean it's safe. You should do whatever you can to give your village what it deserves! It's freedom!"

It was a major conflict, but before she could decide which to listen to, the troll growled "so...you are trying to enter my home?..."

Edna balled up her fists and answered "t-t-th-this is not a h-home, i-its a bridge!" She shouted at the end.

The troll snarled "this is my home you filthy human! And I won't let you defile it with your dirty feet and shoes!"

Edna was getting agitated with this troll, not understanding what his problem was...or his intentions.

Edna stared at him then asked "what do I have to do to cross this bridge? Because I need to get to the other side!"

The troll smiled an ugly smile, but then answered "Don't you worry about that... Because I'm going to EAT you! But, to honor your final wish, I will make sure to toss your bones onto the other side when I'm finished."

The troll took a step closer to Edna, so she had to think of something fast. "No!" She shouted with such confidence and anger, the troll paused.

"uh..No! I-I-I'm t-t-too.." She had to think of something or these would be her last words! "You can't eat me! Because, I am the King's daughter!"

The troll reeled back his claws, slowly. He questioned Edna, "how do I know you're telling the truth?"

Edna hesitated before responding. She didn't have anything of the kings, nor did she even look like him, but she thought of something that could maybe set her free. "I cannot prove that I am the King's daughter..."

The troll scoffed, then proceeded to creep towards her.

"But you can't prove that I'm NOT the King's daughter!"

The troll once more paused. He seemed even more confused.

He shook his head and exclaimed "I know you're not the King's daughter!"

Edna was now just keeping her limbs intact by playing off of the troll's stupidity.

"You believe I'm not the King's daughter, but are you willing to take the risk? If you kill me, my father; the King, will be after your head!"

Edna stood tall, back straight. The troll pondered everything for a while, then Edna decided to take a risk that might end everything, or help everything.

"I have thought of a way to prove that I am the King's daughter."

The troll looked at me with curiosity.

"I will tell you something nobody knows about the King...He has really bad back hair."

The troll looked at her with amusement, but then disappointment. He exclaimed "only a family member would know such things...you may pass."

He stood to the side of the bridge and gestured out to the other side.

Edna hesitantly took a step onto the washed out wood, then ran to the end. She didn't even look back at the troll, her eyes were only on the Palace.

After an hour of traveling, Edna still wasn't even near the Palace. Looking out her window every morning, she knew it was a journey, but she never knew it was this long.

She decided to relax on a tree. She ran out of blue spheres, so she was also hungry and thirsty.

She was so exhausted, she completely forgot about the shadowy figure. So, she went to go find food or water.

She searched for about a half an hour, but nothing showed up.

No blue spheres, no fruit, no vegetables and no water!

She was so desperate, she resorted to eating leaves.

They were refreshing, but the flesh on them was bitter. A little juice dripped on her tongue, but that was it.

She wandered around looking for SOMETHING.

Berries, insects, a puddle! Anything!

It was starting to get dark out, so Edna was getting scared. Not only that she would die of thirst, but that she would die from a wild animal or monster.

She then whipped her head around, checking for the shadowy figure that she reminded herself of.

She didn't see anything suspicious, so she kept searching.

Twenty minutes later she pulled back some branches and what was hiding behind was a miracle. Grey brick stacked upon each other creating the shape of a hollow circle. Two tall, wooden posts were attached to the sides, hanging from the one over the top was a wooden bucket.

Edna took two steps closer, then collapsed at the edge of the well. She managed to pull her dying self up to peek over and see the water.

Once she saw the light sparkle off the glossy goodness that would save her life, she was no longer dry and weak, she had enough energy to leap for the water. Edna grabbed the bucket and dug for the water below. She grasped some, then immediately drank it.

Her back slumped against the stone, while she enjoyed her refreshment. She could feel the cold water go down her throat, bringing to life all of her dead cells.

After finishing the water, she just laid there, finally able to enjoy the beauty of the forest...

CRUNCH! The sound signaled Edna to stand in alarm.

CRUNCH! The sound grew louder as the thing came closer.

Through the brush on the other side of the well, she saw a figure coming closer.

She thought it was the Shadowy Figure as before, but once the creature stepped out into the light, it wasn't what she expected.

"Hehehehe..." The ugly, old woman cackled.

Edna stumbled back in fright, never taking her eyes off the beast.

She knew what it was, but she's never seen one in person before.

Her father once told her a story of a boy who lived in the village. His name was Boyd. Edna's father said he was going through a faze, because he found joy in tricking the village.

The boy was the son of the Dawsons, who owned the sheep farm.

While his parents were gone selling some sheep, he would come running up the hill shouting there was a wolf eating his sheep.

All the villagers would run to his house with their pitchforks looking for a wolf, but there would be no wolf.

This happened a total of three times until the villagers finally stopped believing him.

Once there was actually a wolf, nobody believed him...

The wolf ate all of the sheep and his parents were so poor, they needed to move.

They moved out of the village, but later they came running back saying a witch took their son, but all the villagers thought this is where the child got his lying habits, so they didn't believe... And nobody has seen the child ever again...

Edna tried to run but the witch was already in front of her, not letting her slip away.

The witch showed her claws like the troll did and slowly inched forward. So, Edna tried the same tactic as she tried with the troll.

"I am the King's daughter! Hurt me and you die!"

Edna stood tall and confident. The witch calmed down a bit, causing Edna to believe she won, however all of the sudden, the witch started laughing.

"The King has no daughter! Nobody wants to have a child with him! He loves no one! So, even if you were his daughter, he wouldn't care!"

Edna's heart dropped, the witch was not as dumb as the troll...

The witch snarled "this is my property, little one. My well, my water, now you're my meal..."

Edna must think quickly as she did with the troll, so she shouted.

"I'm not big enough!"

The witch froze immediately. She looked at her with a curious expression.

"You will be just fine." The witch stated.

"No! I won't! You will just be wasting your time, I have nothing to offer. I've been starved for a while now, there is nothing to eat in this forest! If only there was food, even the animals would starve!"

The witch stepped back, with an even more curious look on her face.

"You're right... This is a desolate place. There is no scent to attract my prey..."

The witch vanished into thin air. Along with her, so did the well. Edna sighed in relief, then started back up her journey to the castle.

She almost died twice in one day, she wondered how many more times she could escape, until it was the real thing...

Edna camped out beside a giant tree. She could place her whole body on one root and still have lots of room. She found a little knick that she laid in.

Comfortable, she slept.

A few hours into the night, she heard a growl.

She was asleep, but still alert.

Her heart skipped a beat when she heard the noise.

Wolves? Trolls? The witch found her again? Or maybe something else terrifying... She thought.

She no longer felt comfortable. Instinctively, she decided to look around, make sure nothing was there, maybe just her imagination.

She creeped around waiting for a monster to appear, but nothing did...

She went back to her post in the tree, but when she arrived, she saw something in her sleeping space.

She tiptoed up to the mark on the root. Once she was peering down at it, she knew what it was...a footprint. However, it wasn't hers. Her feet were too small for this footprint. It was maybe slightly larger than her father's.

She looked to the right side of the root. Engraved into the dirt was the same footprint, but it was facing a different direction. Looked as if it was walking away from the scene, but those were the only prints by the one on the wood.

It almost seemed as though the mysterious man fell from the tree, then walked away.

Edna felt a shiver of horror surge through her body.

She then heard a branch snap in the darkness and immediately looked around, fearing whatever was out there.

She felt like running, but the question locked her knees, where would I go?

Run all the way to the palace which was still about fifteen miles away? Or run back home, which was still a long ways away... she was trapped.

Edna decided quickly; due to her adrenaline. She was going to head back home.

Life long trouble was better than no life at all.

Right when she turned back towards the village, something tapped her shoulder...

She turned around, gingerly.

She was now face to face with whatever had been following her.

She screamed the cry of death and fell backwards.

She hit another root sticking out of the dirt, slamming her back into it.

She wanted to cry in pain, but she could only shake in terror.

The monster was no monster at all, but shaped as a man.

He wore a black suit, with scratch marks.

His black hair was messy, but most of it was hidden under a black hat, to go with the suit.

His eyes were as cold as the night air, yet glowed a warming yellow.

His face was dead and pale, never smiled nor frowned, only starred.

She peered up in fright, but eventually she calmed down.

The man didn't even move until she calmed herself. He finally said in a normal voice, "are you finished crying? Or should I waste more time just standing here?"

His voice was actually very soothing. He wasn't a beast, he was just a man, with creepy glowing eyes.

He sighed, "I'll take your silence as a no, I can talk."

Edna adjusted herself on the root, making herself more comfortable. She was very intrigued by what he was going to say.

"I would advise you not to turn back home...you have come too far to head back now. The journey back to the village would be a longer trip than to the castle."

Edna found herself questioning, "how do you know that? How do you know me?"

The man answered "I have been watching you this entire time. Your life has never ACTUALLY been in danger. If that witch or troll got a claw on you, I would have to put an end to them."

Just for a minute he showed his claws, then promptly put them back behind his back.

Edna raised an eyebrow, "wait...why would you save me?"

The man sighed in irritation, "unfortunately, there is someone of higher power than me, and they would like to meet you..."

"Wait, but–"

"Enough!" He shouted in impatience.

He rubbed his nose in frustration.

"I don't have time for this..."

He grabbed Edna by the arm and darted off. She tried to pull away, but his grip was too strong. He also ran with such speed, she didn't have enough time to escape.

In about two minutes she appeared at a log cabin.

It was tucked away between two joining trees. It had a regular sized door that had a small window near the top. The brick chimney on the little roof had smoke blowing out of it.

The Man still didn't let her go, but instead threw her inside.

"Careful!" A mysterious voice yelled.

"Apologies..." The Man exclaimed, with a hint of fear in his tone.

This mysterious voice must have the body of a beast. *Ogre? Giant? Wizard? What could terrify this man?* Edna thought to herself curiously.

She looked around and saw a huge pile of books crowding a corner of the small house.

The fire's light flickered, lighting up the entire place.

All of the sudden, a shadow emerged from behind the books.

It grew larger and larger as Edna's heart beat faster and faster.

The beast was going to appear at any time....what was it?

"Hello!" The same voice yelled. It was high pitched and cranky.

Edna looked around, trying to figure out where it came from.

The shadow behind the books was gone, so where was the beast?

"I said, hello."

She glanced around one more time and saw a tiny, bearded man peering up at her. He was wearing a dark green coat that covered his entire body.

His hair was white and his beard was long enough to touch the floor.

All she could think was...*How does he scare– him?....*

Edna looked over at the Man. She saw him tense up when the little guy looked at him.

She peered back down at the small person, wondering what he even was....

"Hudson!"

"Yes?!" The mysterious man asked in complete obedience.

"Go fetch me the Blood Based Broth."

"Yes sir." Then he darted off.

"Blood?!" Edna gasped in terror.

Nobody answered her. In no time, Hudson was back with whatever the little person wanted.

"Here, sir." As he handed over the small, glass container.

It didn't look like blood at all, it was gray.

The small person nodded, then proceeded to take out more glass containers filled with strange ingredients.

He poured the entire thing of gray blood into a brown bowl, then added a pinch of green, a sprinkle of yellow, a drop of purple and a splash of black.

He then stirred all the elements together, while also blasting a bit of magic from his palms into the pot.

He must be a wizard.... She thought to herself.

As he blended together his strange concoction, the room began to mysteriously dim and almost set into a fog.

"You are travelling through this forest with a purpose, yes?"

The way he asked the question, it sounded rhetorical. She wanted to answer, however her lips wouldn't move more than a shiver.

"of course you are." He exclaimed, "nobody comes through these woods if they aren't looking or wanting something."

He continued, "I have had many people search for me, as well. However, I did not have what they desired."

He poured the liquid into a bowl, "magic is a strange thing. Most believe it will solve their problems, but it will only cause other troubles that they can never solve.

Perhaps, you are a woman so hungry for power, that you leave everything behind to your children, to come to these woods in search of something beyond your comprehension. However, once you finally find it, buried deep into these woods, you become entrapped—never to leave—and that never-ending hunger now craves for something...else."

The room went even dimmer, before it lit up again to it's original state.

"My apologies, I didn't mean to scare you. Magic isn't all bad, though. Good things can spring from it. Like one man who learned sorcery, just so he could be able to enchant some bushes around this forest to grow little blue fruits, so that no traveler must go unfed for days. They turned out quite tastey too."

Edna gulped, looking back on the blue spheres that nearly saved her from starvation.

"Anyway," The wizard mumbled, "what I am trying to get at is... Anyone can do good things, thats easy, but not everyone can do things with good intentions. Selfishness, greed, wrath... Spells reflect it all. But I believe your better than that, Edna."

His words hit like a bird—not the feeling—but the unexpectedness of it, the sheer fluster and confusion.

What does he want with me?... Edna wondered.

He brought the bowl of potion over to Edna with a serious look, but one sniff of that from Edna almost made her gag.

"No!" She yelled.

Hudson was holding her back; so she couldn't run away.

"You must drink it!" The wizard yelled back.

"No! It probably tastes as bad as it smells!"

"Just drink it!"

Just then, Hudson pulled Edna's head back, forcing her mouth open.

The wizard poured the liquid into her mouth and her throat made her swallow.

Once the bowl was empty, the wizard pulled back and Hudson released her head.

Her head bolted upward, and doing so, she spit out whatever she didn't swallow.

"HUUHHH!" Edna gasped for air. Her eyes wide in shock and horror of the taste.

"EW! What was that?!"

The wizard didn't answer her.

"Excuse me, I asked, what was that?!"

Still, the wizard didn't answer her.

"Hey! Little man! Wha–"

All of the sudden, she started to feel queasy.

She thought she was going to puke, but nothing came up.

The feeling grew stronger with each second. She couldn't figure out what it was, but it started to feel more painful than sickening.

She fell onto her palms, but they could only hold her for a second. She grew weak and tired. The whole picture of the room became a blur. A spinning, dark, mysterious blur...

"HHUUUHHHH!"

She shot up, gasping for air.

The pain was no longer present, instead she felt something else. Something that she had never felt before. It was alienating...it was...empowering.

She looked down at her hands.

"AHHHH!"

She turned them over, again and again.

They were different. Her fingers were longer, wrinkled; like her grandmothers. Her nails were long, with shining tips.

Hesitantly, she lifted them up to feel her face. It felt soft, but stretchy and creased.

She shook at the horror of what had happened.

The feeling of a tear rolled down her new skin. It dripped onto her dark skirt.

"Do not freak out too soon." The wizard said.

"WHAT DO YOU MEAN 'DON'T FREAK OUT?!"

She showed him her hands.

"look...I understand why you're upset. But, you won't look like this too much longer..."

He pulled out a gold coin.

Magically, he turned from a short, old wizard, to a tall handsome man.

"Magic..." He explained "Magic can transform you. However, it must come from the right place. Wherever magic comes from, even the heart, it will be fueled with intentions. If your intentions are beautiful, and loving, it will reflect that. But, if your intentions are not—well, you get the gist. "

"Why am I hideous?" Edna asked anxiously.

"That wasn't your spell, it was mine. I guess my intentions were not pure... Which I guess makes sense because it was supposed to make you powerful. And if anything in this world is ugly, it's the lust of power."

Edna looked at herself in the mirror again, and asked "how do I make myself beautiful?"

The wizard held up his gold coin, "you can transfer magic over to an object. If the object is pleasing to the eye, you will be also."

Edna quickly started searching for the object, desperately wanting to turn back.

She went around the room, but laid eyes on something outside.

She opened the door and headed to a rose bush next to the hut.

There was a magnificent rose growing vibrantly.

The Wizard followed Edna out. He watched her peer down at the flower, then asked "is that your object?"

"My mother owns a flower shop in the village. I always loved the roses...."

She caressed the petals gently.

The Wizard saw the emotion between her and the flower, then said "yes, that is your object."

"Just move that warmth you feel to your hands. Then allow the magic to absorb the rose." He explained.

All of the sudden, a golden light transferred from her palms, to the rose.

It glowed and sparkled for a minute, but then all was normal.

"This rose holds power. What you choose to do with it is your decision."

Edna touched the scarlet rose...

The King stood in his castle, admiring the pristine art.

He folded his arms proudly, puffing out his bold chest.

"I will forever reign as the King of this land! Who faces me will crumble just at the sight!" He boasted.

The wind howled outside as the rain poured down the stained glass windows.

Little did the King know, there was one that would not crumble...

Knock knock

The small sound echoed through the empty palace.

Knock knock

The tapping sound annoyed the King, so, he ordered his servant to see what it was.

"Excuse me, your Majesty! But there is a lady here to see you!"

"Send her away! I am busy!" He demanded, but then he heard the woman speak.

"But, I am cold...can you please let me in?"

The voice was of a girl, but when the King saw her, he was horrified at her appearance.

"No! Find somewhere else to stay! There is a cabin a few miles from here!" The King shouted in dismay.

Edna remembered his harsh tone from the village. His greedy expression, when he took everything from people who had nothing! She was giving him one last chance, but he ruined it.

"I had a good heart towards you!" She shouted,

"But that is over now! You have no love in your heart!"

She grabbed the rose from her pocket. Immediately sparks flew.

Edna grew, but changed dramatically. Her hair flowed down her back in a golden glow. Her eyes opened to show blue stars. Her clothes even changed to white robes instead of black.

"I am giving you my rose..."'

A glass vase appeared, then she lowered the flower into it.

"This rose holds much power, however, it is not as lovely as it appears... Every rose has thorns. Every year you do not have love in your heart, the beautiful petals of the rose will fall off, and you will be left with nothing but the thorns!"

"what does that mean?!" The prince cried.

"It means that when the rose withers—your fate is sealed."

The King looked down at his hands. They were large and furry. Long claws grew from the tips of his fingers.

"AAHHHH!" He roared

He hesitantly lifted them up to his face, feeling how much changed.

After a few seconds of complete horror, he yelled again "AAAH-HH!"

Edna glared down at him in joy.

Trying to hide the excitement in her voice, she declared "I will be back when all the petals fall."

And just like that, she left him stranded as a monster, but not before she turned all of his staff into monsters as well.

As she lingered in the darkness of the forest for a moment more, she thought back to what she had just done and wondered if her father would have approved.

Generosity is like a boomerang, he would say, if you throw it out into the wind it will return to you.

Well, I'm sorry father, but the wind can keep my boomerang, because I threw it out for a reason...

She left the palace in search of her village, but when she finally made it back, nobody recognized her.

She decided with the power she now held, she would protect her village from harm.

Maybe one day... She began to think, *maybe I'll see that rose again...*

Chapter Two

Beautiful colors flashed across the sky.

Purple, blue, green, pink, orange, yellow....All of the colors, except red.

The gorgeous little people spreading this delight were called fairies.

This event that had been taking place was called the Parade Of Newborns.

Celebrating the pixies who have just been brought to the world.

Pixies are sent from the stars, then they land in the Crystal Flower in the middle of the Magical Forest.

Every year at the exact time, they travel there to collect and celebrate the New Pixies.

The fairies darted across the sky, trying not to be late for the coming of Pixies.

Far away to the north, sparkles were shooting down from the atmosphere.

"Go, Go!" a little purple fairy cried. "We'll be late! We'll be late!"

"Be quiet, Penny!" An orange fairy demanded. "The Elder fairy will hear you! You know she is already stressed!"

"About what?" A blue fairy asked.

The orange fairy rolled her eyes. "Didn't you hear? One of the stars that the pixies came from exploded."

"Really?!" A green fairy overheard. "But, that only happens every million years!"

A yellow fairy shushed them all, knowing that the Elder had already heard them.

Finally, the fairies made it, only seconds before the hatching began. The colors were flashing everywhere and the crystal of the flower made them shine everywhere.

It was said that if you were watching the sky as this was happening, that you could see the clouds reflect the rainbow glow.

"Aawwww!" A little pink fairy squealed as one of the pixies was being born.

"Oh yes, you haven't seen a hatching before, have you, Ava?" The Elder Fairy asked.

Ava shook her head no, not wanting to take her eyes off of what seemed like a miracle.

"Well..." The Elder fairy began, "since you seem so attached to this one, you get to name her."

"Really?!" Ava shrieked in delight. The Elder nodded.

"Hmmm... since it's a beautiful green fairy, I'll name her....Fern."

"What a gorgeous name!" The Elder declared.

The Elder looked over at the Fairy, Eleanor, and asked her to name the blue fairy that just hatched.

"Alright, I'll name her...MaryWillow."

"Wasn't that your caretaker's name?" A yellow fairy named Debra asked.

"Yes, yes it was..." Eleanor admitted "And I will take as well of care of MaryWillow as my caretaker did for me."

Fairies nodded in respect, as they watched their pixies being born.

All of the shells glowed with what color of fairy the pixie would be. Except for one.

One that was placed in the middle, not having a single crack in its shell, even though all of the other pixies hatched.

The Elder looked down at it curiously, then gasped "huh! How dreadful!"

All of the fairies looked at her shocked, "what do you mean?" Some of the fairies asked.

"Uh-uh-huh, This pixie is...dead!"

"What?!" All of the fairies gasped in unison.

The Elder's assistant fairy flew over to her, stunned. "B-b-but, no pixie ever dies! At least not in their shell!"

"I know!" The Elder stated, "but that's the only explanation!"

When the Elder says that, it has a different effect. No fairy doubts it, what the Elder says is truth and no fairy can say otherwise.

The assistant fairy picked up the egg and carried it to the field.

Every fairy said their goodbyes, but before she dropped it, the egg started to glow.

It glowed a strange color, that the fairies have never seen a fairy glow.

It was the color of war. The color of what stained the swords and teeth of enemies. The fire of which homes and castles were destroyed. No fairy of good was ever supposed to shine this color....red.

The shell cracked and wiggled in the fairies hands.

Pieces fell out into the fields below, until there was nothing left but a red pixie.

Every fairy stared at her, not sure what to do.

Then...it yawned.

"AHHHHHH!!!" screamed all of the fairies from their dead stares.

The assistant fairy didn't know what to do, holding such a creature.

Her mind forced her to drop the unknown beast, for who knows what it was capable of?

"No!" Shouted a blue fairy, on her way to save the little pixie.

The pixie tried so hard to use her wings, but that takes practice.

The blue fairy dove as fast as she could to save the little one, but she wasn't fast enough.

So, she did what she had to, even though it was strictly forbidden. She used whatever magic power she could conjure up to save the pixie.

Not knowing exactly what would happen, she did whatever she could.

Thankfully, it was actually helpful.

Vines covered in flowers shot out of her wand to catch the pixie.

"Haa," the fairy sighed in relief once the vines caught her.

The vines rolled up to bring up the shaking pixie.

"There you go." The blue fairy stated as she slid the newborn pixie into her hand.

All of the other fairies flew down to her in a stern manner.

The Elder Fairy glided right next to the blue fairy and said "of course you saved her."

After a tense moment, the Elder Fairy declared "since nothing like this has ever happened before, we will handle this by Fairy Law."

"Whomever is the first to care for the pixie right after hatching, will be responsible for the pixie until after the Ceremony Of Magic."

The Elder Fairy looked down at the red fairy in disgust, "but since she is taking care of such a creature, I as The Elder Fairy, for as long as I reign, will not allow this...this...THING, into the Magic Courts!"

All of the fairies gasped.

"And I believe you all know what that means, but I'll say it anyway, this Thing will not be allowed to participate in the Ceremony Of Magic!"

All of the fairies looked at each other, not knowing how to respond.

The Ceremony Of Magic is a right of passage for fairies to start using their magic gifts. and for a fairy to be expelled from the Ceremony Of Magic is unheard of.

"B-Bu-But, please, Elder, you can't do this to the poor pixie. Magic is the only thing to protect fairies from predators...."

The Elder Fairy turned to her with a horrid smirk.

The blue fairy looked down at the red pixie in a motherly manner.

"It will be okay, you're in good hands." The blue fairy said gently to the red fairy, but by then the red fairy had already fallen asleep.

The blue fairy looked down at her in compassion, "my name is Eliza, but, I'll name you...Rose."

"Fly Rose! Fly!" Eliza was shouting up in delight when Rose learned to use her wings.

"I'm doing it! I'm really doing it!" Rose shouted back.

"Don't go too high, Rose!" Eliza warned.

But, Rose didn't listen, she was too excited.

She flew up above the trees into the beautiful sky, however, it only seemed delightful and peaceful for a little while.

She heard the flapping of wings that could never come from a fairy, but it sounded familiar.

She stopped accelerating and just floated there, looking around for what was causing the noise.

"CAW!" She turned around and a bird was flying towards her.

Its black, crazy eyes darted around, and huge wings flapped with such thrust, it didn't take long until it was inches away.

"AHHHH!" Rose screamed and then dodged, only centimeters from its mouth, but the gust of wind that came from such large wings projected the small fairy off into the forest below.

As she was falling, the fairy realized she couldn't keep her balance or the tension that helped her fly.

She was fighting, but that only made her spin more, she was trying to get her wings straight, but that only made her twirl.

She was tangled in her own helplessness.

She eventually landed on a leaf from a tree, but, with such force from the fall, it bent and she hit another leaf. She kept rolling off the leaves until she finally reached ground.

"Ouuuuucc Hhhh" She groaned as she tried to get up. Her vision was blurring and her head was pounding.

She looked over her shoulder and saw her bent wing.

She tried to straighten it out with her hand, but before she did she heard someone shout "no!"

She quickly looked up in fear of another bird.

"Don't do that!"

Rose's head darted around like the bird's eyes, trying to see who was shouting.

She eventually saw a blue blur in the distance.

In hope that it was her caretaker, Eliza, she tried to stand in greeting, but as the blue blur got closer, she saw it was not Eliza.

Rose sat in disappointment, leaning up against a tree.

She waited for the blue fairy to come closer, but Rose knew what the blue fairy would do...She would take one look at the color of her wings and fairy dust and fly away. Who could blame her? That's what all the other fairies did....

"Hey! Are you okay?!" The blue fairy yelled in concern.

Rose rolled her eyes, "I'm not a pink fairy!" Rose responded, remembering how other fairies sometimes thought she was pink at a distance.

"What?!" The blue fairy asked in confusion to Rose's response.

Rose waited for the blue fairy to turn around and never come back, but she didn't.

She kept coming closer...and closer...and closer...until she was right in front of Rose's face.

Rose looked her directly in the eyes and said "what are you doing?"

The blue fairy peered down at her and replied "don't touch your wing. You might rip it."

Rose looked back at her wing, only for a second though, because something wasn't right.

"Hey, Fern!" yelled the blue fairy, "come here!"

"Coming!" replied another voice.

Rose shifted herself closer to the tree.

Within a few seconds a green fairy appeared.

"Oh my!" Fern, a green fairy gasped. Rose nodded to herself, because that was the same reaction many other fairies have had.

"Your wings!" Fern added.

Rose's eyes shot to look at her in shock.

Were these fairies color blind? Rose asked herself.

"What can we do to help, MaryWillow?" Fern asked.

The blue fairy, MaryWillow, answered "well we can't bring her to the fairy hospital...."

"Oh yes, we mustn't." Fern agreed.

"And why is that?" Rose asked, even though she already knew the answer.

Fern hesitated to say, "well....I don't know if you know this but..."

"You're red." MaryWillow stated.

"Well of course I know that!" Rose yelled, "so why are you helping me!?"

Fern and MaryWillow looked at each other confused.

"Because you're another fairy..." MaryWillow explained.

"I know that...." Rose grumbled, "but every other fairy screams at the sight of me...so why aren't you two?"

MaryWillow giggled at her face when she grumbled and of what she thought was a ridiculous question, but in all seriousness, Fern answered "Even though you are a different color of fairy, even though you didn't come from the same star, doesn't mean you aren't a fairy, and doesn't mean you didn't come to this world at the same time as us. Technically, we are sisters."

She looked at both of them, in a loving expression.

"Okay, okay! Enough with the lovey dovey!" MaryWillow declared, "we have to fix her wing!"

While Fern and MaryWillow were talking over what to do, Rose was holding back tears. She has never been called a sister before.

"Alright! Here's what we got!" MaryWillow proclaimed.

"We are going to use magic!"

"No!" Fern yelled, "that's not what I said!"

"Don't care!" declared MaryWillow.

She placed her two hands on Rose's bent wing, "now..I've never tried this before...but, back at Magic Academy we've learned some kind of healing spell."

"No, we didn't." groaned Fern, "that was a re-creation spell."

"Same thing!"

"It's really not."

"Hang on!" Rose demanded, "just what kind of spell are you doing?! I just learned to fly and I have so much more I want to learn. And I need to get home. I don't want to be a red fairy along with being a ground–"

There was a blue flash, then all went silent.

Rose cautiously looked over her shoulder at what MaryWillow did.

When she saw she gasped "huh! You fixed it!"

"I knew I could!" MaryWillow boasted, looking up at Fern mockingly.

Fern rolled her eyes, but then said "we better get– this fairy –back home."

Realizing she never gave them her name, Rose quickly proclaimed "Rose...my name is Rose."

Rose eventually made it back home, but, didn't see Eliza anywhere.

Rose had said her goodbyes to Fern and MaryWillow when she could find her way back, so Rose was all alone.

She decided she had enough with nature for one day, so she locked herself up in the small cabin Eliza built.

Rose expected Eliza to be back soon, but the hours came and went, so did the night.

Rose could hear the wolves howling and the birds cawing. Twigs snapping, winds blowing, trees shaking.

It had been like this every night, the only thing different is Eliza was nowhere to be found.

Rose tried to calm herself down to rest, but her fear kept her awake.

After she heard a crow caw for the third time, Rose decided to go look for Eliza.

Rose gingerly opened the door and cold winds rushed at her instantly.

"Bbbrrrrr," murmured Rose as she stepped out into the darkness.

She thought of flying, but she wasn't good enough to do it in harsh winds. She could barely stay on the ground!

She started running in the direction of the Fairy Palace, to see if Eliza was there.

Rose knew very well she would not be welcomed, but that didn't mean she couldn't sneak in.

She was out in the wilderness for hours. Freezing and tired, she thought she wouldn't make it.

Eliza always warned her not to go out at night, that there were dangerous creatures that wanted to hurt her, but she couldn't stay back, Eliza might be in trouble!

"CAW!" she heard in the distance. Even the sound of it made Rose freeze in her tracks.

She looked around, but couldn't see anything. She then snuck into a crevice of a tree, and waited.

In her waiting she couldn't help but cry.

She didn't know where she was going, she's never even been to the Fairy palace. She wanted to head back but she didn't know how.

She was lost, and there wasn't anything she could do...

"Hey? Do you hear that?" A voice said in the darkness.

"Yeah, I think it's coming from over there." A voice responded.

Rose's head shot up in hope, but then down in misery. Anybody who saw her wouldn't help her...

"Huh!" the same voices gasped.

"Rose?!" they both said in unison.

Rose looked up, seeing the colors of the fairies.

"Fern?! MaryWillow?!" Rose exclaimed gratefully.

They ran to her in delight, but also confusion.

"Did you get lost again?" MaryWillow asked.

"Kind of..." Rose admitted.

"How?"

"well...I'm looking for Eliza..she's my caretaker...I haven't seen her at all."

The two fairies scratched their heads.

"Well...do you want us to help you find her?" They asked.

"Oh yes! That would be wonderful! I actually think she is at the Fairy Palace! Do you two know where that is?!"

Fern and MaryWillow both looked at each other painfully.

"Well...you see Rose..." MaryWillow tried to explain. "We're lost!" cried Fern, "when you found us— or we found you, we were trying to find our way home! Because we both flew off when we learned how to fly! Then we went too far! Then we got lost! Then we got tired and went on foot! Then we found you! But you weren't from the Fairy Palace! So when we got you back home! We've just been out here forever!!!" Fern sobbed, but MaryWillow had no part in it. "Stop crying!" MaryWillow yelled, "The monsters will find us!"

"Maybe I want the monsters to find us! Put us out of our misery!" Fern wailed.

Both MaryWillow and Rose stepped away from Fern, realizing she was serious.

"It's okay, we can help each other find the Fairy Palace." Rose exclaimed.

"*Sniff, sniff*, really?" Fern asked.

"Yeah!" Rose said, kind of excited.

They all agreed they would find the Fairy Palace, so they took off.

They flew in an educated guess direction. They have been flying for about two days, but never seemed to find another fairy.

Since they were young and just learned to fly, they had to take breaks now and then.

Eventually, Rose shouted "hey! Look! Is that it?!"

Fern and MaryWillow stopped. "YES!" they screamed in relief.

"Finally! We're home!" They both exclaimed.

They could see the peak of the fairy palace. The top where it was in the shape of a cone.

They flew with all of their energy until they could see most of the palace.

It was all of the colors (except for red), with swirling golden designs climbing up the sides.

There was a great, wide balcony that neared the cone shaped top.

The entrance to the balcony seemed to have no doors, it was open space, but there were pink curtains tied to the sides of the entrance with golden rope.

"Why is that necessary? It's huge!" Rose exclaimed while pointing to the enormous balcony.

"Because that's where the Elder Fairy makes all of her announcements." Fern stated.

Rose rolled her eyes, "this Elder Fairy sounds pretty important. I hear Eliza talking about her all the time. Like, how she's so unreasonable and mean."

"SHHHH!" both Fern and MaryWillow spitted.

"Why?" Rose asked.

Fern and MaryWillow looked at each other in fear.

"Because we might not be alone. And the Elder Fairy is GREAT-LY respected. If she finds out we were talking about that she could...she..."

Fern and Merryweather shushed themselves before they could say it. Not because what they were going to say was wrong, but because it was too much to handle at such a young age.

Rose rolled her eyes again, "you two worry too much."

Rose flew past them, but before she could go any further, Mary-Willow grabbed her.

"No!" She demanded.

"What?" Rose asked.

MaryWillow's grip grew tighter, "you can't go any further."

"Why not? I have to find Eliza."

"Because...if you get caught...you see...how do I put this...you.."

"...wouldn't be liked..." Fern said in a low and shy tone.

Rose laughed at them, "you don't think I know that?!" She looked at them both. "Of course I know that! I'm not an idiot! But I have to find Eliza. I'll just sneak in, nobody will notice me."

Before either of the two fairies could say anything, Rose had already flown off.

As Rose got even closer, she saw what circled the palace.

Beautiful lights hung in the trees, with colors swirling all around.

She could hear singing and smell a scent that was unfamiliar, but delightful.

She wanted to soar down and play with the other fairies, but she knew that would be the worst mistake she could ever make.

Instead, She flew down to a tree in the forest that surrounded the whole palace.

There were no lights or glowing in this tree, so she thought it would be fine.

Feeling tired once she reached it, she laid on one of its branches. She was so determined to find Eliza, she didn't realize just how exhausted she really was.

She listened to the sound of music coming from the joyful fairies. She closed her eyes and let out an exasperated sigh.

Her mind went blank and she dozed off.

"GET HER! She doesn't belong here!"

Rose's eyes popped open, ready to defend herself.

When she abruptly stood up in a fighting position, she saw nobody around her. She didn't even see anyone coming toward her.

She peered around to see what all the commotion was about.

Through the thick trees, she saw what seemed to be a human.

Rose had never seen a human before, but Eliza told her about them.

From what Rose remembered, she could tell that this human was not of regular size. When Rose curiously moved closer to get a better look, she could tell it was a girl.

She had very long brown hair and was wearing a blue dress.

She saw male fairies chasing her, with swords (since male fairies don't possess magic).

"Get her!" They ordered, while trying to slash their swords at her back.

"No!" The girl screamed, "I'm just trying to help!"

Rose flew down closer to the chase, until she saw a blue glow coming from the girl's hands. Curious at what it was, Rose moved dangerously close.

She saw blue sparkles coming from the girl's hands, but, still didn't know what it was, so she decided to follow.

"Nevermind men!" A powerful voice declared, "come back to the palace!"

Immediately, the male fairies turned back.

The little girl, even though free, never stopped running.

Rose knew she couldn't last much longer in the air, so, found a resting spot in the girl's lowered bonnett.

Rose woke up from a deep sleep once again.

This time, she was in a soft place, with a view of a beautiful garden.

"It's okay now, you're safe."

Rose turned to see who said that, but, then remembered she was in a little girl's bonnett.

"Thank you, but I didn't need your help."

Huh! Thought Rose, *Eliza?*

Rose climbed to where she could see.

Eliza was frowning down at the garden.

Rose wanted to shout "I found you! I found you!" but didn't.

For some reason, something was telling her not to.

So, she just listened to Eliza talk...

"I was fine in the cell." Eliza exclaimed.

"That's nonsense! Who's fine in a cell?" The little girl expressed.

They both chatted for a moment, then Eliza said "well...I better be going... I have..ehe em, a lot to do."

The little girl bowed her head, "Like what?"

Eliza tightened her fists, "just stuff, ok?" She replied sternly.

The little girl replied with the same look, obviously making Eliza uncomfortable until she spoke.

"She's dead!" Eliza yelled, trying not to sob, "Sh-She was taken! She's gone!" The tears rolled down her face whether she wanted them to or not.

Before Eliza could cry in front of the little girl anymore, she left.

Rose was stunned, silent and motionless.

She thought I died? Rose asked herself.

Rose wanted to soar up to the clouds, find Eliza and hug her, but before she could, she heard the little girl say to herself, "who died? Could she still be sad about her caretaker's death?" Those words made Rose freeze. *Eliza's caretaker died?*

"Wouldn't she want to talk to me about it?... Nevermind, she's been too busy ever since she took on that pixie... too bad she never has time for herself anymore to gather her thoughts..."

Rose froze. *She's right.... The human's right.... Eliza never has time for herself... She's sad about me, but I'm the problem! I got her band from the Fairy Kingdom! I made her an outlaw! She suffers because of me!...*

Rose balled up her fist and declared to herself. *I'm old enough to take care of myself! ... for Eliza's sake....*

The little girl stood up.

Rose slid into her bonnett again, still wondering who this little girl was.

After a little while, a new castle emerged in the distance. It was much larger and looked older than the Fairy Palace.

It had golden looking brick and pyramid shaped tops.

After a while we got closer to the castle. About a mile away, the little girl stopped. She then ordered someone, "take me to the castle, please."

A masculine voice replied "yes, Princess."

Rose's face dropped, *this girl is a princess?!*

The girl hopped into a carriage and almost squashed Rose when she leaned back into the seat.

Rose was bouncing and shaking up and down as the carriage navigated through the woods.

Eventually, the carriage stopped and the door opened.

A gentleman helped the princess out of the carriage and onto the path that led up to the castle's grand entrance.

"Thank you, Benjamin." The princess said in a mature voice.

"At your service, my princess." Benjamin said with a bow.

The little princess started her way up the path, but Rose wanted to look around.

She flew out of the bonnett and to an open window in the castle.

The window she chose was a hallway window, so she followed the hall.

The floors were made of glossy white tile and the walls were pink and...red, decorated with drawings of red roses all around.

Rose eventually reached a hallway that had pictures of Queens and Kings.

She even found a nice portrait of the little princess. The smile the princess gave in the picture was contagious. It even made Rose smile through her grief of losing Eliza.

Rose shook her head, trying not to get too hung up on that. Every fairy leaves their caretaker at some point, just usually not so soon.

Rose wiped away a tear that slipped out.

Just then, she heard a noise coming from further down the hall.

A door opened, but before Rose could see who was behind it, she hid behind a lamp shade.

"Come on, I think I saw her go this way." A voice whispered.

"No, it was the other way!" another replied.

Rose sighed in amazement and just plain exhaustion, because she knew who those two voices belonged to.

"Ouch! MaryWillow!" Fern shouted/whispered.

"Shush Fern! You're going to get us caught!"

Rose slid from behind the lamp shade to face them.

"Hhuuhh!" gasped Fern, "I told you!"

MaryWillow rolled her eyes, "hey Rose, glad we found you."

"How did you find me?" Rose asked.

"We followed you when you flew away and were following that girl." MaryWillow explained.

Rose looked at them confused, "Why in the Fairy world would you follow me?"

The two fairies looked at each other, just as confused as Rose.

"Because we wanted to help you...." They both said slowly.

Rose looked at them back and forth, but before she could ask why, she heard someone coming down the hall.

"Okay, okay, whatever! You're already here! Now just hide!" Rose ordered.

They all flew further down the hall, away from the echoing footsteps.

They found a red door on the right side of the hall, so they decided to go in it.

Once they were able to open the door, they slid in, but it was very dark and none of them could see.

"Turn the lights on!" MaryWillow shouted.

"Ouch!" Fern whined, "something hit me!"

"Sorry!" Rose admitted.

Finally, Rose found the light switch.

When the lights came on they noticed they were in a completely empty room, except for a pink, closed curtain on the wall across from the door.

Rose flew up to it curiously, then peeked behind it.

It wasn't like she expected. It was more of a window than a hidden portrait.

However, the window didn't look out into nature, it looked out into a massive room.

The room had sparkling tile floors and small indoor balconies looking over it. Up on the ceiling three, great big, golden chandeliers hung. The light from them reflected off of the floor and shimmered in the whole room.

As the fairies stared in amazement at the glamorous room, they noticed two people walking into the room.

It was a woman along with a man.

The woman had brown hair; a lot like the Princesses hair. Her skin was pale looking, but her face seemed to have a warm glow. She was also wearing a simple dress, but elegant. It was purple with jewels lining the V-shaped neck.

The man on her left side also had brown hair. He was tall and nicely groomed. He was wearing a white turtle-neck shirt with a long black coat draped over.

Rose strained herself to listen to what they were talking about, but they were too far away.

"AAAAHHHHHHHH!!!" screamed Fern from over by the door.

"What?!" Rose asked loudly while turning around.

"AAHHH!" Rose screamed too.

There was a man trying to snatch MaryWillow who was blasting blue dust at him.

"Get away!" Both Fern and Rose yelled.

Both Rose and Fern tried to help MaryWillow get away, but before they could, a net was thrown at them by the man.

They all got tangled up in the rope and couldn't escape.

The man picked them up and carried them to the other side of the palace.

Once they reached a brown door, the man stopped.

He politely knocked on the door with one knuckle. A second later, the door opened. The Princess was behind it, gesturing to the man to come in.

The room was decorated with pink walls and beautiful drawings of nature scattered along them.

"There you are!" the Princess expressed when she knelt down to look at them.

"Oh look! You look a lot like Eliza!" the Princess exclaimed when she pointed to MaryWillow, "What's your name?"

MaryWillow looked at her disturbingly, "what's your name?" She scoffed.

"Oh me? My name is Lily."

Almost immediately, Rose had a flashback...

"Where are you going?" Rose asked. Eliza looked at her, "oh, I'm heading out to visit Lily."

"Who's that? Is she another fairy?"

"Sure." Eliza responded. Then flew out.

Now that Rose thought of this, she realized Eliza went to meet Lily a lot more than she once thought.

"How did you know Eliza?!" Rose blurted.

Princess Lily looked at her startled, "oh, Eliza, yes, you must be –Rose! Oh my goodness! I didn't see you come in! I only saw these two sneak in."

Both Fern and MaryWillow blushed in embarrassment.

"Why are you here?" Lily asked with a concerned tone.

"I'm not totally sure myself... But, how do you know Eliza?"

"Well..." Princess Lily continued, "I've known her ever since she was a pixie. I was about...six years old at the time, now I'm twelve, so we've known each other for a long time. You see, Eliza was never the best behaved fairy...she was more of a troublemaker. She always used her magic when she wasn't supposed to, and went past the Fairy Flying Boundaries a lot. The Fairy Council was going to suspend her from her studies since she was always getting in trouble, but, it's a fairy law that the fairy or the fairy's caretaker have to be there when they force the suspension, but since Eliza's caretaker died...Eliza decided she didn't want to go, so she flew away. Later, she found me. I was playing in the garden and she asked for water. I gave her water and we just became fast friends. The rest is history." Princess Lily smiled warmly at Rose.

"Oh..." Rose replied, realizing why Eliza chose to be her caretaker.

It was because Eliza understood what it was like to be an outcast...

"Ummm so speaking of water...can we get some?" MaryWillow asked.

"Of course. Faris, can you go and fetch some food and water for these fairies?" Princess Lily asked the man.

"Your wish is my command." Faris replied with a chuckle under his breath.

He rushed out to get what the Princess ordered, then a few minutes later came by with fruits and vegetables.

"Forgive me Princess, but I don't know what fairies eat..."

"It's alright, Faris, this will do." Princess Lily stated.

Once they all finished their snack, Princess Lily wanted to show the fairies something she found.

"It's right along here, I buried it." Princess Lily announced.

Princess Lily knelt down to dig, but Faris stopped her. "No Princess. I will not have you digging in the dirt."

"Ugh, Faris! You've been so overprotective lately!" Princess Lily accused.

"I stand by my words." Faris affirmed.

He dug for about five minutes before reaching what was hidden.

"There it is!" Princess Lily announced happily. "I haven't seen it in a long time."

Faris handed her a black, but, shiny object.

"This is what I wanted to show you." She held it up high for the fairies to see.

"What is it?" MaryWillow asked.

Princess Lily lowered the object and looked down at it. "This is a piece of an enemy."

"What enemy?" Rose asked curiously.

"The enemy of Darkness. She is like no other. We call her a Fallen Fairy." Princess Lily explained.

"What's a Fallen Fairy?" Rose asked.

"She is only half fairy– from what I've heard anyways. Apparently her mother was a fairy, but her father was a monster."

"What do you mean monster?" Rose inquired.

"I don't exactly know...All I've ever heard was monster..."

Rose scratched her head, trying to picture what this "monster" would look like.

"Anyway," Princess Lily continued, "She was half fairy, half monster, so she wasn't allowed to be a part of any Fairy schooling, or events."

Hearing the story of the Dark Fairy, Rose started to feel sympathy for her, understanding how hard it is to be an outcast.

"But, surprisingly, she was never upset about it. She actually didn't like fairies that much, so she was pleased not to be a part of them."

Rose's head popped up. *What? I would give anything to be considered a normal fairy, but she didn't even care?* Rose once felt sympathy for the Dark Fairy, but now she couldn't care less.

"Sadly, she was orphaned at a young age, and because she was all by herself, she had no one else to communicate with, except for nature. But, according to Wiser's, not all of nature is good. There are spirits. Some are good...and some are evil. Unfortunately, she became friends with the darker spirits..." Princess Lily stopped there. It must have been all she knew.

"Anyway, this is a part of her horns, it got chipped off a long time ago." Princess Lily carefully placed the piece of horn back into the ground.

"Excuse me, Princess?" Faris asked politely. "But don't you have classes to get to?"

"Oh shoot!" Princess Lily exclaimed. "I have to get to class! My apologies, fairies, but Faris can let you go now!" Princess Lily said in a hurry. She ran to the east tower in a panic, leaving the fairies with Faris.

"Well, I guess that means we can go, let's go, Fern." MaryWillow ordered.

Right before Rose was ready, Faris called "Rose? Can I speak with you? Just for a moment?"

"Sure." Rose replied.

She flew down and sat in his open palm to rest.

"What's up?" She asked.

Faris looked down on her, intensely. "The Dark Fairy is not done."

Rose's eyes shot up to stare at him. "What do you mean? Why are you telling me this?"

"Listen!" Faris yelled, startling Rose. "The Dark Fairy isn't done! She has never been after the fairies...she's always been after the Royal family."

"But why? What does she have against the Royal Family?" Rose questioned.

"It's because... Princess Lily's father...killed the Dark Fairies father..." Faris answered reluctantly.

"B-B-but why?!" Rose asked, shocked.

"Because..like Princess Lily said..he was a monster. The King ordered for him to be killed before any attacks were made by him. You must understand! It was for the safety of our kingdom!"

Rose couldn't look him in the eyes after he told her they created an enemy for no reason.

"But..this isn't about the King's decision and safety, it's about Princess Lily's safety."

Rose peered up at him again, "how?"

Faris looked down at the ground in shame, "I have a terminal illness. So, I only have so long to live."

"What?" Rose gasped.

"Please, let me finish quickly. You are the fairy of Eliza, a fairy who protected the Princess for many years. So, if I had to choose anyone to protect my Princess from The Dark Fairy, I would choose you."

Flabbergasted, Rose couldn't find a way to respond correctly.

"U-um-umm...I'm not sure. I can't even use my magic yet. So, I'm sorry, but I think you chose wrong.."

Faris chuckled under his breath, "no, I do not believe so. You may not be able to utilize your magic yet, but, I do believe in time, you will be perfect for the task."

"You don't understand! I'm not just another fairy. I don't go to Magic School or anything else for that matter. I have no experience with anything dangerous except for a bird! And-and-" Rose was about to break down in tears, but stopped herself.

"I know you don't believe in yourself, and that you don't think I know about you, but trust me I do. Princess Lily has thought I am ignorant about Eliza and you, but I'm not. Like I said, I protect the Princess, so I must know where she is all the time. I know all about you and your red color, but, to be honest, that's part of the reason I chose you."

Rose looked up at him with teary eyes. She has never known her red color to do anything but get her into trouble. Never in her life did she think someone would pick her because of it.

"I want you because, even though you aren't great with magic yet, you are..different and special. Even I, a human, can tell you will possess great power one day and provide more protection for the Princess than I ever could."

Rose's tears turned to pride and joy. She has never felt so honored and needed than she did now. All her life she felt as though she was a burden, everybody just waiting for her to pass on, but now, she knew she was meant for so much more than that.

"Alright!" She agreed in a prideful tone, "I'll do it, but not only will I always protect Princess Lily, but I will guard and fight for her descendants as well!"

A year later, Faris passed away.

He was buried in the forest next to a river in honor.

Rose, Fern and MaryWillow came to his funeral to pay their respects, and Rose knew what she had to do.

"Queen Lily has given birth to a princess!" shouted the King to his people after a long day of birthing.

"We will hold a grand party to welcome her into this world!" He announced to the kingdom.

"MaryWillow...Since you're the strongest in magic, I want you to go last giving your gift...just in case." Rose ordered.

"Understood." MaryWillow agreed.

Chapter Three

"Excuse me, Sir David? Have you found my caretaker, Beth, yet?" Eliza asked worriedly.

Sir David sighed, "no, Eliza, we haven't found her yet."

"But she's been gone for two days now! How have you–"

"Eliza! We are searching! I'm sorry, but just let it go!"

Eliza scoffed in hatred, then flew away back to her home.

She looked out of the window in her home. The view was of the deep forest, lush greenery, fruit hanging from the trees... but her caretaker was out there and they weren't doing anything to find her.

She trudged around home, bored and worried. So, she decided to do something about it.

Eliza grabbed her flashlight, cloak, food and water, but there was one more thing she needed...a wand.

She couldn't really use it, but just in case, she would bring one along.

The only problem was, she didn't have one.

After graduating Magic Academy, you finally receive a wand to control your magical power, the problem was Eliza hadn't graduated yet.

She knew where the wands were kept, but it would be a risk to try to get one.

Eliza flew out towards the Fairy Palace. She pictured in her mind where the wands were located. A carved wooden box in front of a stained glass window. The polished carved wood sparkled many colors from the light that shined through the colorful glass.

Once she reached the Palace, she tried to slip through the side window. Unfortunately, one of the male guards caught her.

"Hold on! Where do you think you're going?"

"I–um–" She couldn't think of anything before the guard took her away.

"Go back home! If you try this again, I will report you to the Fairy Council."

Eliza flew back, but when night time hit, she decided to try again.

This time, she used a hidden entrance that was farther away from her target.

The entrance was covered in hay and moss, but she easily dug through it.

The door leading to the basement of the palace was made of wood, but is so old that it was mostly rotted.

She quickly swooped down to the abundant basement, then carefully found her way into the actual palace.

The inside of the palace was full of gold and silver, it decorated the walls and floors.

There were many doors to different rooms inside the palace. Many staircases to explore, but Eliza had her eyes set on one room, a room that was so plain you would never expect such important objects to be stored there.

Eliza only knew of this room because of Beth. Beth used to work for the Magic Academy, and knew about all the secrets. She wouldn't tell Eliza most of them, but some were bedtime stories.

Eliza hurried up two staircases in the south tower, through three halls enriched by portraits of past Fairy Leaders, but beyond that, the map in her mind went blank.

Dang it! She thought to herself. She was disoriented by the two paths to choose from. *Left or right?!* She asked herself in panic.

Sadly, she eventually chose left on a guess and made it to two white doors. Without thinking, she flung them open expecting to find a wooden carved box in front of a stained glass window, but instead, she found an elegant staircase leading to a ballroom, filled with fairies from the Fairy Council.

Dang it... She again thought to herself.

Eliza was returned to her home with an escort, Paula Green; A fairy council member.

"Eliza? What were you doing in the palace?" Paula asked as she flew Eliza home.

Eliza ignored her interrogation. Instead, Eliza was thinking of a new plan to get into that room.

Once they reached Eliza's home, Paula left.

Eliza thought all day about how to get into the palace, then she finally figured it out.

"Hey, Jessica?!" Eliza shouted to a pink fairy picking fruit.

"Oh, hey Eliza! What's up?" Jessica replied.

"Uh, I have to tell you something."

"Oh yeah? What is it?"

"Well, Beth always puts on the Fairy Council Feast...You know, for...Good luck!" Eliza came up with it on the spot.

"Really?" Jessica responded questionably.

"Oh yeah, they have them all the time. Beth used to do them...but..." Eliza made sure to almost shed a tear, which wasn't hard, because she felt like crying all the time.

Jessica looked at her empathetically, "ok..yeah, I think putting on a feast would be fun! Actually, I bet the cooks could get it done in time for tomorrow!"

"Great.." Eliza said while holding a grateful smile.

The next day loads of delicious food was being brought into the palace. The Fairy Council was staring down from the huge balcony in delight.

Jessica did tell the Fairy Council it was a feast for good luck. They were slightly confused, but who cares as long as it's a celebration with yummy food?

While all of this was happening, Eliza was getting ready to sneak into the palace to steal the wand.

When 7:00 pm hit, everyone was in the dining room to enjoy their feast.

Since all of the Fairy Council members were in one room, that's where all of the guards were.

Eliza was able to get in through the west side, but the wands were in the south side.

Eliza quickly took all of the halls and, carefully this time, doors to get to the south side.

Eventually, she finally made it to the right room. She knew it was the right one because Beth had described it to her once. A door that is too plain to think there could be anything important behind, but once you open the doors, you find yourself in a room glowing with different colors, because of the stained glass window that was placed behind a beautifully carved box.

Eliza cracked open the door and the colored moonlight pierced through.

Eliza sighed in relief, then went into the room. There was indeed a beautifully carved wooden box in front of a stained glass window, but there was something she did not expect. The carved box was entangled by iron chains. There was a specific lock that dangled from the chains. Eliza gingerly touched it to see if somehow she could pick it, but unfortunately, it was a magic lock that could only be unlocked by a specific wand. Obviously the Fairy Elder's wand.

Eliza tried to smash it with a rod she carried with her; just in case, but the iron rod didn't even scratch it.

Just then, she had an idea. She wasn't good at using magic yet, but she knew she had some–because she always got in trouble for using it.

Eliza concentrated on the metal chins that were blocking her way. She concentrated on the idea that nobody even tried to find Beth. The fact that Beth was missing even though she said she would be back at midnight six days ago!

She felt the magic power flow through her body in a matter of seconds. She had no idea what her magic would be because she's never practiced the actual thing much.

BAM! A loud burst echoed through the palace. "Shoot!" Eliza shouted when she saw what happened.

The flowers around the room wrapped around the box with a magic glow.

ERRR. ERRR. ERRR a deafening sound came from the box. The chains were glowing red and then she realized, it wasn't only a magic lock, they were magic chains to detect outside magic!

She heard yelling voices from the guards getting closer and closer.

Eliza decided to ditch the wand and go find Beth without it.

She looked around for an escape, but there were no windows and only one door, where the guards were coming through. So, she went through the only exit she could, the stained glass window.

She smashed through it and flew as fast as she could out of sight and out to find Beth.

After about a day of flying, Eliza had to rest. She found a comfortable spot under a bush.

Eliza ended up passing out, but after about an hour, she heard yelling and the sound of horses running.

"Heeyah! Heeyah!" Men's voices shouted while they whipped the horses to go faster. The horses naying echoed through the woods, as if they were screaming for help.

The noise grew louder as the herd got closer.

Eliza crept further into the bush, scared of whatever it was. *Did the fairies hire humans to catch me?* She thought for a brief moment, then realized that fairies would rather die than ask for human assistance.

The noise eventually revealed itself to be a black carriage, being pulled by two horses.

As the carriage passed, Eliza noticed something. Purple sparks flying out of the open window.

Eliza remembers them immediately, those are Beth's sparks! Eliza rejoiced in her head.

She quickly tries to follow the carriage, but ends up losing it because of exhaustion.

She knelt on the dirt path in shame. She lost Beth...again.

After a few minutes of regaining energy, Eliza started flying upwards.

If there was a fancy carriage, there had to be a fancy castle.

She peered into the distance in all directions and squinted to see a kingdom many miles away, to where it seemed like a blur.

"Yes!" Eliza exclaimed to herself.

After another ten hours of flying and quick rests, Eliza finally made it to the castle.

It was a wide and gorgeous castle, reaching up to the sky to look down upon the village that thrived there.

There were many guards and walls to block out any unwanted visitors, but they were no problem for Eliza; since she was so small.

She circled the giant castle to find Beth, but she didn't see any more clues.

Once she reached the East side, she heard an angry voice.

"I want her dead!" The voice yelled in frustration.

Eliza abruptly stopped when she heard this.

She gawked into the window where she saw a tall, dark haired woman wearing a long black dress with a high crown.

"I want her gone! I want her killed!" The woman screamed in exasperation.

She was circling the room, but whenever she screamed she was looking in a certain direction.

Then, Eliza heard another voice coming from inside. The voice was a low pitched one, calm and rhymed.

"Don't be so fast to kill the King's daughter, for there is a certain time for slaughter."

The woman tightened her fist, "you are useless! All you tell me is to be patient!" The woman threw a glass vase onto the floor and called "little fairy!"

Eliza's ears popped up once she heard the calling. Before she could see the voice's face, the tiny, frightened voice asked "yes, Your Highness?"

"Fix this broken thing. I want a new one that gives me good advice!" The woman ordered.

"B-Bu-but Your Highness, I cannot do that. The spell can only be used once, I'm sorry but enslavement spells are tricky that way..." The frightened voice replied.

"Then do a repair spell." The woman snarled, "Fix it, or die."

The fairy quickly revealed herself so she could do another spell on the strange voice.

It's Beth! Eliza shouted in her head.

The little purple fairy aimed her wand in a certain direction.

Eliza shifted so she could see what Beth was doing.

Through the window, hanging up on a wall was a foggy, ornate mirror. The cloudiness in the center formed the shape of a face. A pale, expressionless face.

BLAM! A golden spark flew from the crystal wand to the mirror. Purple waves moved across the mirror until they disappeared. After a few seconds, the cloudy face re-appeared.

Beth moved aside as the dark woman walked closer to the mirror.

"Now...crystal mirror on the wall...Who's the fairest of them all?"

Without hesitation, the mirror replied, "you, My Queen."

Beth rolled her eyes away from the mirror, shamefully.

The Queen shewed Beth away. Beth quickly flew out of the room, so Eliza followed her.

She watched Beth go a little ways until she was stopped by human guards. She then proceeded to reluctantly follow them.

They led her down many hallways and a few flights of stairs until they reached a small, dark room.

Once they locked the doors, they walked away.

Eliza swiftly made her way through tiny areas to get to the locked door. Once she made it, she knocked. *KNOCK, KNOCK,* "Beth? Are you there?" Eliza asked hopefully.

"Eliza? Is that you?" Beth responded.

"Yes! It's me! Open the door!"

"I-I can't."

"Why not?"

"Because the door is locked, so I CAN'T get out!"

"Okay, okay, let me try something."

"Wait-wha–"

Eliza couldn't hear what she said because she backed up to try a spell.

Alright Eliza, you got this. Eliza told herself.

She felt the power flow through her veins. The aching in her head, to the tingling in her toes.

Her hands tensed up, then she thought, *OPEN!*

Instantly, the thorny bush that was yards away from the locked door moved its limbs into the keyhole. Eliza watched in amazement as the limbs wiggled around for a few seconds.

The door creaked open, but Beth didn't rush out like Eliza thought she would.

"Beth?" Eliza asked as she moved closer to the door. Eliza peeked inside the tiny room until she saw Beth up against a wall.

"Beth? Why aren't you coming out?"

Beth looked at Eliza, with a hint of fear in her eyes.

"I-I can't..." She muttered.

"Of course you can!" Eliza exclaimed, "come on!" Eliza tugged on Beth's arm to get her out of the room, but Beth struggled. "No Eliza!" Beth shouted in a harsh tone, "I can't escape! I'm in too deep! This woman is a monster and if she sees that I'm gone she will hunt down the fairy kingdom and kill every fairy! I'm sorry...I just can't..." Near the end Beth broke down in tears. Eliza let go of her arm and watched Beth sink to the floor.

"I-I under–" Eliza started to say, but decided against it, "No! I don't understand! You are a strong fairy and agreed to raise me until I was old enough! But guess what? I'm not old enough! So you're going to raise me until I'm just like you!"

Beth peered up at her like she was crazy, "are you stupid or just THAT obnoxious? Didn't you hear what I said? Fairies will die if I come back! This isn't just something I came up with to get rid of you! It's life or death, so if that means I must give up myself for you and other fairies, then I will!" Instead of tears she scowled at Eliza, stubbornly.

Eliza stared at her face for a few seconds, trying to let go...But just couldn't do nothing.

"But there is something you could do..for me." Beth stated.

"What?" Beth asked, in a tone that already agreed to whatever task is being presented.

"There is a princess, her name is Snow White. Her father sadly passed away...But it wasn't an illness like her stepmother said, secretly, the stepmother killed the father..."

"Huh! That's awful! Why would she do such a thing?!" Eliza gasped.

"That is not your concern. What you should be wondering is how to help Snow White escape." Beth stated.

Eliza looked down at her questionably, "Escape? Why would I help her escape?"

"Well the question 'why' is simple, because I told you too! And how...that's for you to come up with. I just want this girl to be safe.

She is young and sweet, doesn't deserve being locked up in a tower..."
Beth looked up, even though there were no windows.

Eliza could see her sadness and frustration. "okay...I'll do it..." Eliza muttered. She couldn't speak higher than that, because the sorrow made her want to burst into tears.

She wanted to tell Beth about everything, and how she could never return to the Fairy Kingdom, but there was no time. Both of them heard rattling and voices coming from outside the door. Then Eliza realized the door was still open! She peaked her head outside and saw guards running towards the jail cell.

"You must go! Before they catch you too!" Beth shouted.

"But I don't want to leave!" Eliza responded in grief.

Beth stared at her for a few seconds, then Eliza left. She flew through the door and to an open window. She took a deep breath of cold, bitter air. The stabbing feeling in her throat tightened, so she didn't even want to breathe. Her wings failed to give her flight, so she landed on the freezing grass.

She heard the clattering inside from the guards. They were yelling at Beth to never try and break free again. They slammed the heavy door, locking it behind them and leaving with their loud metal feet.

Eliza looked off into the distance. The hazy sun hid behind the clouds, wanting to be left alone. The sky looked gray, along with the dead willow trees, still hanging just for decoration.

The smell of the air was dry and cold, but the place itself felt inviting and comforting.

Eliza curled up in the moist grass, waiting for nothing, except the release of the lonely pain.

"Oh, beautiful shadows so high in the sky! Show yourselves proudly, for you are the reason WHY!" A gorgeous voice sang from an unknown location. Her voice echoed through the dark and gloomy garden.

Eliza looked up to wherever the lovely voice was singing from. She saw a tall, gray tower on the western side of the castle. Birds were flocking the small window that opened the peak of the tower up.

Eliza flew up to the window surrounded by birds, but right when she reached it, the birds fled.

Eliza saw no head beside the opening, so she turned her teary eyes to the inside of the room.

There she found a bed with a golden spread. Alongside that was a tall and wide dresser, filled with gowns. An oak door was located on the other side of the room, supposedly leading to the stairs, but the most lovely thing of all in this room was the princess brushing her hair in the mirror, humming to her own song.

She had long black hair and pale skin. Her eyes were bright green and her lips were blood red.

Eliza hid behind the stone wall, surprisingly scared of being seen.

All of the sudden, a voice came calling from outside the door, "Princess? The Queen has requested your presence at once." The small, fragile voice squeaked.

The princess's head jerked to look in the mirror. The expression on her face was no longer a joyous one, but a fearful one.

"Coming." The princess responded, reluctantly.

She quickly finished smoothing out her hair, then stepped out into the hallway.

Eliza felt the urge to follow her, so she did. She followed her down four flights of stairs, then through dimly lit hallways, until they reached a corridor.

The princess stepped lightly into the room.

The Queen and her fake, but wicked smile turned to face her.

"Snow White! Darling! How's the tower?" She asked in an obviously phony, nice voice.

"It's nice..." Snow White responded in an inferior tone, not looking her in the eyes.

"Excellent!" The Queen exclaimed, then proceeded to stare at Snow White. "Darling, I wanted to address the issue about men writing to you." A snarl slipped out when she said this.

Snow White clutched her hand, looking even farther away, "It's just sort of a royal thing, I am almost of marrying age..."

"You're sixteen!" The Queen shouted, trying to sound motherly, but it turned out envious.

"I-I apologize..." Snow White replied to the harsh tone, "I didn't mean for any trou–"

"Enough!" The Queen interrupted, "I have already ordered the guards to take care of this mess. There will be no more letters."

"Yes, Your Majesty," said Snow White.

"Please..." The Queen started with a taste of cruelty in her voice, "call me..mom."

Eliza noticed right when the Queen said that, Snow White's fist instantly tightened and her jaw clenched.

"You may leave now." The Queen instructed.

Snow White silently nodded, and followed a maid up to her quarters in the tower.

Eliza didn't follow her this time, she was too shaken up by that scene.

They barely even look at each other... Eliza thought to herself with a distaste in her mouth, but before Eliza could fly away, she overheard the Queen and a man talking.

The man was tall and lean, dressed in black with red, slicked backed hair.

"I order you to get rid of her tonight, I can't stand looking at her face! Can't stand knowing she's up in the tower like a portrait for everyone to see!" The Queen roared while pacing back and forth.

The man just watched her, quietly.

"I want you to take her out to the forest, kill her there..." The Queen looked directly at the man, with her cold, dead eyes, "and bring me some of her remains...just so I know it's done..."

The man gulped, showing some resistance, "Of course Your Majesty, anything you ask..."

The Queen peered at him for a moment more, then turned away.

Must have been a que for him that he could go, because he rushed out.

No! I can't let this happen! They can't kill her! Eliza thought, then also remembered what Beth told her, Help Snow White escape. So, Eliza decided sooner was better than later.

Instead of going to Snow White, Eliza decided to go to the man she saw planning with The Queen.

She found him in a tiny office, wandering the walls, mumbling to himself.

She tapped on the window with her small fist. The second she did so, the man's head spun around to acknowledge her. First he gasped, then fell on his butt, then got up and asked through the glass, "who are you? What are you doing here?"

"My name is Eliza, and I'm here to help Snow White." Eliza replied loudly so he could hear her.

"What? What do you mean to help her?" He questioned in a fully knowing tone.

"I saw how you looked when you were ordered to kill her...I know you don't want to." Eliza explained.

"You got it all wrong! I was just pondering how to kill her." He said, lying through his teeth.

Eliza stared him down until he finally admitted, "ok, yes! I don't want to kill her! I am loyal to the throne...And even though The Queen is upon it, she is only a placeholder!"

The man said it with such a disgraceful look on his face, directed both at the Royal Kingdom and himself.

He pondered his selfishness for a moment before Eliza said "If you want to do the right thing, then help me save her from being killed!"

The man looked at her blankly, just staring. He blinked twice, then shook his head rapidly. "Alright! I'll do it! But...how? I'm supposed to bring back evidence..."

"Leave it to me!" Eliza declared.

Eliza went straight to the butchers shop and stole all of the meat and organs she could. The whole time she was replaying the memory of Beth, lying on the floor, broken...

She stuffed the cow organs into the bag, then hurried out.

It took her a while to get back to the castle, with all the weight holding her back.

She eventually made it back, but before she came through the window to the man, she heard voices inside.

"I'll handle it, Your Majesty." She heard the man's voice say.

"You better, but I want it done before midnight, understood?"

"Yes, Your Majesty."

She heard the door open, but before she heard it close, the Queen added something, "oh, and, Hanbert, don't forget to fetch me my ice chips." Then the door closed.

Hanbert...that's his name.... Eliza peeked through the window and saw it was clear.

"Hi...." Eliza squeaked. She saw Hanbert sitting in a chair against the wall, holding his face in his hands.

"Is everything ok?" She asked gingerly.

"Yeah, I'm fine..." He groaned, "just...scared." That word seemed to have killed something inside of him. His eyes were dim, weak, sad.

"I–I got the..stuff.." She presented.

"Good, good, now, we have to get this done fast."

Hanbert turned to the only witness in the room; a maid that was standing near the door and told her, "please, go fetch me Snow White and tell her the Queen would like to see her in the garden."

Eliza went to the garden to prepare.

Once Snow White arrived, Eliza made herself glow a bright blue.

Snow White was so intrigued, she followed Eliza into the woods.

"Wait! What are you?" She asked curiously, "where are you going?!"

She had such a calm and kind voice, just like when she was singing.

When Eliza met Hanbert at the spot in the woods, she stopped glowing. Eliza looked up at the castle and saw a spec that must have been the Queen, waiting to hear a scream from an innocent girl.

Snow White gasped when she noticed Hanbert standing there with a bag.

"P–Pl–please don't!" She pleaded, knowing he was ordered to kill her.

"Shhhhh!" He shushed, "I'm not going to hurt you!"

But that scream was perfect to satisfy the anticipating Queen.... Eliza thought to herself.

"W–What?" She asked with tear stained eyes.

"I was ordered to kill you by the Queen, but I'm letting you go. She is envious of your beauty. She's obsessed with it! Now go! Leave! Run as far as you can!" He explained.

She stood there, dumbfounded. "B–but this is the only home I've ever had...I can't leave it..."

"No! You must! For your survival!" He shouted quietly.

"N–no... I'm heading back.."

She turned around and started to walk back, but Hanbert grabbed her and put a knife to her throat from behind. "Leave, or I'm going to kill you here and now." He muttered with a growl.

Snow's body went numb, then turned back around to run away.

Once she was out of sight, Hanbert fell to his knees.

Eliza went up to him and tried to comfort his shivering body.

"I can't believe I put a knife to the princess's throat!" He cried, "I promised her father I would protect her! But I threatened her!"

"You did protect her!" Eliza comforted, "she's safe now."

Once Hanbert felt better, they went back up to the castle, carrying the bag of cow organs.

Eliza waited outside the window of the Queen's bedroom as Hanbert presented the organs.

The Queen didn't want to touch, or even look at them for very long, so she didn't notice the difference between species.

"Wonderful, good job Hanbert, that girl will be no burden any longer." The Queen said while applying a cleansing face mask.

Hanbert left her room and Eliza followed him.

She caught up with him when she reached the first open window.

"Why are you still here?" Hanbert asked when he noticed Eliza, "Your job is done."

"I know...but I was wondering if you could help me with something?" She asked.

"Like what?" He stopped and turned to face her.

"My caretaker...she is locked in the jail cell three floors below. I want her freed." Eliza answered.

Hanbert's head jerked away. He made a disappointed sound.

"What's wrong?" Eliza asked worriedly.

"I–uh–I–I can't help you with that." He rubbed the back of his head shyly.

Eliza lowered herself to the floor, hopelessly.

She felt the tears prick her eyes until they hit the marble floor.

"Why not?" She grumbled.

"I'm so sorry, but that would surely get me killed. I don't want to die."

She looked up at him grudgingly, "I helped you, why aren't you helping me?"

"Your life wasn't on the line! If I help you free a prisoner...they would be after my head!" He pleaded.

She regained her flight and yelled "you useless coward!" Once she yelled this, she flew away, out of the castle, out of the court yard, and out of the kingdom.

She wandered around for days, until she finally found another castle.

Nope! She declared to herself and found a beautiful garden instead.

She picked berries for her lunch and petals for her torn clothes.

She relaxed in the garden, under the sun.

"Haaaa" she sighed to herself.

"Haaaa is right!" She heard a voice say.

She immediately popped up, scanning the garden, until she noticed a little human girl. She had brown hair and blue eyes, and wore a pretty pink dress, with a pink bow in her hair to match.

"Hi!" She squealed happily.

"Uh–hi." Eliza responded awkwardly.

"Wow, I've never seen a fairy before...you're gorgeous!" The little girl exclaimed.

"Oh–well–thank you." Eliza blushed as she touched her hair, not knowing how to talk to this girl.

She seems sweet... Eliza thought, while peering down at the girl.

"My name is Lily! What's yours?" Lily smiled up at Eliza eagerly.

"Uh–my name is Eliza." Eliza stated.

"Pretty, I like that name."

Not long after that, Lily and Eliza became good friends.

They made a pack to visit every week at the same garden, and they always did.

Eventually, after some hard effort and a lot of service, Eliza was welcomed back into the Fairy Kingdom.

She never told anybody about what happened to Beth, she decided to leave it as a mystery.

Eliza never got another caretaker, since she was approaching age to be let go, and because she never wanted anyone else.

Years came and went, until it was time for Eliza to join the other fairies in the Parade Of Newborns.

This meant that Eliza could finally become a caretaker, even though she didn't really want to be one.

During the parade, Eliza was talking to the fairy she was flying next to; a yellow fairy named Sandra.

"Come on Eliza, what fairy doesn't want to be a caretaker? It's literally a stage in our life, kind of like wrinkles." She said while looking at the Fairy Elder, disgusted.

"I know...But raising a pixie is just a lot of work that I don't want to deal with. I'm just going to be on the side watching miracles being born and hope they don't tag along with me." Eliza said with a chuckle.

"Ugh, whatever, I'm just hoping I get a blue pixie, they're just naturally laid back." Sandra proclaimed.

"Thank you." Eliza responded.

"yeah...You're the exception..." Sandra said, with a straight face.

When they reached the Crystal Flower and witnessed the falling eggs, they just waited, waiting for the last egg to fall.

Once the last egg fell, they all swooped down and watched all of the eggs hatch.

"How cute!" One fairy shrieked.

"Adorable!" another cried out.

Like Eliza said she was going to do, she waited at the side.

Every other fairy was too excited to notice her not participating, so she was good until...

"This pixie is dead!" The Elder shouted.

"What?!" All the fairies cried while they circled around.

Eliza couldn't help her curiosity, she had to see what was happening.

The egg was resting in the middle of the Crystal Flower, motionless.

It had no crack, no movement, no glow, nothing.

"That's the only explanation!" The Fairy Elder announced.

Eliza gawked down at the egg, feeling empathy build up inside her.

Before she could reach out, the Fairy Elder's assistant grabbed the egg and hovered it over the field. But, thankfully, before she could drop it, it wiggled, then glowed a color that did not exist in a fairy, or at least wasn't supposed to.

It glowed red.

The egg burst open, revealing a happy looking, red, pixie. It cuddled into its half broken shell and yawned.

Eliza looked at it joyfully, even though it was strange, but then, everybody screamed bloody murder.

Out of panic, the Fairy Elder's assistant dropped the pixie.

"No!" Eliza yelled as she saw the poor pixie fall.

Without hesitation, Eliza did whatever she could do to save the pixie. Eliza knew this would be the last straw for her, but she couldn't let the pixie die.

She used her magic to catch the pixie, having flowery vines shoot out of her wand.

"Gotcha." She sighed in relief as the pixie landed in the flowers.

She gently pulled the pixie up, cupping her in her hand.

"It's okay, it's okay," She tried to sooth as the pixie was shaking in fear.

The Elder Fairy creeped up behind and said "of course you saved her..."

After an intense pause, the Elder Fairy declared "since nothing like this has ever happened before, we shall handle this matter by Fairy Law."

"Whomever cares for the pixie right after hatching, shall take care of that pixie until the Ceremony of Magic."

The Elder Fairy glared down at the red pixie in disgust.

"But as long as I, Fairy Elder reign, I will not allow this...this...THING, into the magic courts!"

All of the other fairies gasped.

The Elder Fairy smirked in an evil way that reminded Elize of the Evil Queen, "and I believe you know what that means..."

After the male fairies issued everyone else to go home, the Elder Fairy muttered into Eliza's ear, "I know you know that becoming that pixie's caretaker was the last straw. The court and I were going to let all of the illegal stuff you committed slide, but now, we don't even want you back..."

Those words sparked an anxious terror into Eliza's stomach, but when she looked down at the red pixie, who was no longer afraid, Eliza wasn't either.

Eliza flew off with the pixie in her hands. She remembered her home in the Fairy Kingdom. The stone walls in her small house, which was sitting in a tree. All of the other fairy houses surrounded hers. The laughs, the twinkling sounds, beautiful colors flashing all around. Even though the fairies angered her with their ignorant ways, she was going to miss it.

She was hovering over the endlessly stretched forest, searching for a place to call home.

Eventually, she found an open space. She quickly flew down and relaxed on a log. The trees enclosed the space, making it a part of the dark forest.

She looked around the log, making sure that it was clean and suitable, but there were many holes that were able to let predators in.

She thought real quick what she could do, then grabbed her magic wand.

The log turned, shifted, folded, then curled, creating a cute little house.

Eliza flew in, checking the place out. It was very comfortable and safe, along with being spacious, however, it was still just made of nearly rotten wood.

Years went by. Eliza continued to visit Princess Lily every once and awhile, but Rose kept her busy.

Rose was growing rapidly, but was still a small fairy.

One day, Eliza thought it was time for Rose to learn how to fly.

"Okay, Rose, make sure not to fly above that tree." Eliza pointed to the tall tree ahead of them.

Rose flew up and felt the wind on her face. The smell of the leaves on top of the trees were surprisingly sweeter than on the ground.

Rose was so used to being small, but now she was on top of the world...so she wanted to go even higher.

She flew a few inches above the tree...then a little higher...than a little higher.

Eliza yelled "Rose! No!", but Rose was not listening.

Eliza didn't see it at the time, but a bird was headed Rose's way. Before she could see it, it was too late. The bird sped into Rose.

All Eliza saw was a red spark, falling into the woods.

She immediately flew up over the trees, trying to find Rose.

She frantically searched into the trees, on the ground and into any log. She still couldn't find Rose.

"Rose!!!" She screamed in panic.

She searched for a whole day, but before she gave up, she thought of something. *The Fairy palace! There is a Fairy Council member who can see BEYOND.*

Her exhausted gaze turned up to the sky. Then, Eliza remembered what happened when she visited the Fairy Palace after she took in Rose....

"Who said you could come back here?" A fairy asked harshly when Eliza was headed to her old home.

"I just forgot some stuff." Eliza said while trying to get past the fairy.

"Well, I'm sorry but your home is now owned by another fairy." The purple fairy stated in a "get out of here" manner.

"What do you mean another fairy lives there already? The Fairy Elder told me I could get my stuff this exact day!" Eliza explained.

"Oh, yeah, that's why she had me stationed here, I'm supposed to tell you that the Fairy Council decided that you're no longer welcome here. And to make that even more clear, your stuff was thrown out."

Eliza's fist balled up, tight. She was imagining the sweet feeling of punching the purple fairy square in the face, but then remembered Rose. If she assaulted another fairy, she would surely be sent to jail, Rose would be forced to survive on her own...

So Eliza decided to take the high road, and fly away, never to return again...

While Eliza was returning to the exact place she never thought she'd see again, she knew she would be asking for trouble.

That purple fairy's face still endlessly angered her.

Since Eliza already knew the direction of the Fairy Palace, it only took her four hours to get there.

Once the Palace came into view, it almost looked like the Palace where Beth was held against her will.

The memories darted through her mind, giving her a cold chill, but this was the only way to find Rose.

She hurried as fast as she could to the Fairy Palace, trying to be as sneaky as she could.

Her head was kept on a swivel, making sure there were no fairies watching. If one saw her, they would definitely recognize her; since Eliza was only one of two fairies to have been cast out.

She was headed to the secret entrance, under the old, abandoned wheat.

She dug through the wheat to finally reach the hidden door underneath.

She lifted with all her might, and luckily managed to get it open.

She swiftly flew through to find herself in the same dark basement.

She wondered why the Fairy Council never did anything with this part of the palace, because it was a large space.

Eliza saw the glowing crack of the upper entrance to the palace. It was the only light that shone in that room, except for the quick moonlight that flooded the room when she opened the outside entrance.

Once she got out of the basement, she looked for...

oh what was the name... Eliza thought to herself, stopping in her tracks.

Was it... She pondered, then finally, accidentally, shouted out loud, "Navy the Navigator!" She clasped her hands over her mouth when she said it. *Shoot!* She thought.

Then she heard a rumbling from down the hall, making her have a flashback from when she was caught last time.

She quickly tried to find a hiding place, but there was nothing in the hall. No portraits, desks, vases, plants–nothing! She then decided to fly the opposite way, but quickly realized the footsteps were coming from the way she came, so she wasn't anywhere she recognized.

Still, nothing to hide behind, instead, it was a wall. She was trapped in a dead end.

The footsteps grew closer and faster, until a shadow draped over her like a big blanket on a humid day.

"Hey! What are you doing here!?" A male fairy yelled.

Eliza turned around, to finally face the end of the road. She couldn't get any more grace from the Fairy Kingdom, at this point, it was time for the fairies to become more merciless than the red they despised.

The male fairy grabbed Eliza's arm and escorted her to the Fairy Council.

When they entered the large courtroom, the Fairy Council was already seated, waiting.

Eliza was set behind a wooden desk, awaiting her punishment. She looked up at the Council. They were seated in a row, one in the middle and three next to her, seven in total. The colors were patterned pink on the far left, next; orange, yellow, middle was the green Elder Fairy, then on the Elder's right hand side was blue. Next to blue, was purple, then on the far right end was....white. The only white fairy known in the Fairy Kingdom. Her name was Navy; Navy the Navigator.

The Elder Fairy spoke first, "Eliza...what a...pleasure...it is to see you again. If only it was under better circumstances."

Eliza rolled her eyes while biting her tongue, to keep herself from saying something that will make this even worse.

"So...let me first ask...why are you here? I mean, don't you have a little...red fairy back home?" The Elder Fairy asked with a snarl, trying to look as cheerful as she can in front of her "audience".

Eliza curled her fist, then looked up at Navy, while resisting the urge to cry, "I need to know where she is!"

After a few moments of Eliza's silence, The Elder Fairy repeated "So? Why are you here?" This time with impatience.

Eliza's stare moved to face the Elder Fairy, then responded with a slight growl, "She is...fine." Half lying, and half trying to comfort herself for the time being.

"Well, that still doesn't answer the question; why are you here?"

Eliza thought for a moment, because she forgot to think of a lie.

"I–I'm here..because.." Her voice drifted off, trying to use this moment to get free and get what she wanted.

"..I'm here for Navy the Navigator." She stated.

The Fairy Council turned to look at Navy, who still held that blank stare, with those foggy eyes.

"Navy, is this true?" The Elder Fairy asked.

Navy not only can navigate anything, but she can see into the past, present and future; although she refuses to tell anybody what will happen...

I know she knows why I'm here...come on Navy, give me a chance... Eliza pleaded in her head.

Everybody waited in anticipation for Navy to answer.

"I have no business with this fairy." Navy declared in a flat, emotionless tone, while staring dead ahead at Eliza, never blinking.

Eliza balled her fist in frustration, *what...*

"You heard her! This fairy has no business here! And she has come into our kingdom unannounced and unwanted. Guards!" The Elder Fairy smacked the desk in front of her, not needing to, but wanting to.

Guards immediately grabbed Eliza's arms, pulling her out of the courtroom, down multiple halls and stairs, until they reached the murky prison.

The guards opened the squeaky, heavy cell door, then flung Eliza inside, quickly closing it.

They never said anything, only gave her a disgusted glance then moved on.

Eliza searched around her cell for anything to get herself free. She even tried to use her magic, but not only were there no living things down here to use, the cell bars seemed to absorb any magic power.

"UUGGGHHH!!" Eliza groaned in frustration.

After about an hour of exhausted attempts to free herself, she heard the upstairs door open, then promptly shut. She heard a few footsteps on the metal staircase, then saw the white figure.

The room was dimly lit with two flickering oil lamps, but that white figure stuck out like a meadow in the middle of a desert.

"Navy..." Eliza murmured curiously, but Navy did not respond in any way, as if she was asleep.

After a few moments of engrossed silence, Navy finally said "I refuse to help you."

Eliza's hope and heart sank, "why?"

Just then, Navy's eyes became cloudier, as if a storm was rolling in.

"You destroyed my caretaker's sacred stained window!"

Eliza was startled, not just because she learned that the window belonged to Navy's caretaker, but because she had never heard even the slightest emotion pierce Navy's words, until now.

"I–I–eh–I–" Eliza stuttered. "That was an accident...I had no other choice..." She peeped out.

"No other choice?! Why were you even in there?" Navy snapped.

"I–I–It was for my caretaker..." Eliza answered.

The clouds in her eyes rolled out a bit, "your caretaker? Beth?"

Eliza slumped down on a ledge of concrete in her cell, already expecting Navy to know all about Beth and what happened.

Then all of a sudden, Navy muttered "let her go..."

Eliza's head popped up, "what does that mean?"

But before Navy answered, she was gone.

Eliza shook the locked door, "Tell me what that means!" She screamed, "or at least get me out of here!" She screamed in an agonizing tone, "Navy! Tell me where she is..." Her voice died off. She stopped shaking the bars and instead knelt to her knees...

"Tell me where she is!"

The sound of Eliza's own voice echoed through her head.

The memory of standing in the corridor yelling at a few of the Fairy Council members.

"We don't know!" They told her, but the next part was what almost brought her to tears, "...just let it go..."

"Honey! You must finish your studies!" Queen Ruby yelled to her step-daughter, Princess Lily, who was running out of the palace.

"I know!" Princess Lily replied, "I'll be back soon!"

Princess Lily jumped over the old, short teacher trying to grab her and take her back. Then proceeded to run past the guards, who were stationed at the gate, and make it to the dirt road leading the kingdom.

"Stop her!" The old, grumpy teacher shouted to the guards.

The guards immediately started chasing her, only to lose her when she made an abrupt turn into overgrowth, which stretched along both sides of the road.

After a few meters of intense, scratchy overgrowth, she made it to the secret path. The path was a drawn out one, that was enveloped in short, perfectly green grass.

Lily galloped about a mile, then finally made it to her garden.

The garden was abandoned a long time ago by some farmers, who had to sell their land to afford their sons medical fees. Apparently, he and this girl ...*oh, was it his sister or girlfriend?* Princess Lily had to ask herself, forgetting that part of the story.

Anyway, he fell down the hill that was all the way in a distant view.

However, for some reason, the people who ended up buying the farm totally forgot about the garden, and let overgrowth enclose it so it stays hidden.

But, the amazing thing is, the garden itself is still beautiful. It grows many roses, daisies and even tulips. It also grows vegetables and fruits, but Princess Lily never eats those, unless she's starving.

Princess Lily collapsed happily in the garden, right beside the rose bushes. Roses were Princess Lily's favorite flower, ever since she was told the story of her great uncle, Prince Of The East, and his wife, Beauty.

Princess Lily was staring up at the sky, *it's so bright...* She thought.

"Lily..." A majestic voice whispered.

Princess Lily shot up and looked around to see who was there.

"Lily..." The voice whispered again.

"What is it? Who are you?" Princess Lily demanded.

"Eliza is in trouble...the Fairy Palace..." The voice then died off, but led with a strong wind that made Princess Lily turn in the direction of the Fairy Palace.

Eliza in trouble? What kind of trouble? I thought humans weren't allowed in the Fairy Kingdom? But if there is one thing Princess Lily knows, it is that when a mysterious voice tells you to do something, you do it.

Princess Lily ran to the stables and before she got caught by the Horse Keeper, she grabbed her horse, Casper.

Casper was a slick, white horse, with an attitude to other people, but kind and gentle with Lily.

"hee-Yah!" Princess Lily proclaimed to Casper.

The horse then galloped and turned wherever Lily steered. It was strange, but a map had formed in a brain that she had never seen before, leading her to the Fairy Palace that she had also never been to before.

The wind flowed through her long hair, and kissed her face.

She hadn't been in the real forest for so long, she had forgotten how sweet and refreshing the air tasted. The joy of jumping over the fallen trees and ducking under low branches.

"Run, Casper! Run!" Lily cheered.

Five hours later, she found herself at the edge of the Fairy Kingdom. The actual palace was still three miles away, but she decided to leave Casper there.

"Sorry, Casper, but I don't want to risk you squashing any fairies."

Casper snorted, but understood.

Lily headed deeper into the Kingdom, keeping her head on a swivel at all times.

Luckily, once she finally reached the main area of the Kingdom, all of the fairies were celebrating elsewhere. She heard the song, "Happy Birthday", break out, so it must have been some fairies birthday.

Lily crept behind a huge tree, and peaked her head to see if anyone would see her.

"HUH!" Lily heard a voice behind her gasp.

She shot her head around and saw a yellow fairy, carrying a cake, staring at her in disbelief.

She saw the fairy take a sharp inhale, getting ready to scream, but Lily slapped the little cake out of her hands, and grabbed her in a fist.

She made sure not to harm the fairy's wings, but to make sure the fairy didn't scream, she covered its mouth with her thumb.

"Shhhh." shushed Lily, "I'm not here to cause trouble, I'm just trying to find a friend...Her name is Eliza, do you know where she is?"

The fairy struggled in her grip.

Lily carefully took the fairy into the woods, where none of the other fairies were.

"Alright, I don't mean to sound evil here, but nobody will hear you scream, not with that music playing... So, answer my question, do you know where Eliza is?"

Lily gingerly took her thumb off of the fairies mouth.

"Pe-pe," the fairy coughed in disgust, "I-I don't know..."

Lily sighed in frustration, "well do you know what might have happened to her? I got a strange message that she was in trouble, and in the Fairy Palace."

The fairy thought for a moment.

"The Fairy Palace does have a prison, but that's only used for...invaders..." The fairy looked straight into Lily's eyes.

"Then she must be in there!" Lily exclaimed, sort of nervously.

"G-great, can you let me go now?" The fairy urged while shifting in her fist.

"No, sorry, I can't, I let you go once I get Eliza, but I'm going to need your help."

"Uuuggghhh."

Lily placed her thumb back on the fairies mouth, and headed for the palace.

Good thing Lily was a small child, or she wouldn't have been able to fit.

She had to slightly crouch, but it wasn't bad.

"alright...Um...what's your name?" Lily asked the yellow fairy.

Reluctantly, the yellow fairy answered, "Iris."

"Wow, that's a cool name! I'm Lily."

Iris smiled up at Lily for the first time, with a warm chuckle.

"Alright, where do I go from here?" Lily asked.

Iris looked around, "I don't know, regular fairies aren't usually allowed in the Palace."

"Hmmm, well at our palace, the prison is in the basement." Lily thought out loud.

"Wait, 'our' palace? As is yours?" Iris questioned.

"Yeah, I'm a princess, Princess Lily."

Before Iris could express her amazement, Lily started for the west hallway.

"What are you doing?" Iris asked nervously.

"I just thought of something. The kingdom I live in was the first one built, the palace has barely changed over time. All other kingdoms and palaces are sort of replicas of ours, with only slight differences, But the architecture should be about the same."

Lily snuck through the west side, made her way down four flights of stairs, until she reached a tiny door that she could not possibly fit through.

She kneeled down and looked through the opening, and saw metal stairs that surely led to the prison.

"Ok, Iris, I need you to go in there and get Eliza." Lily ordered.

"What?! No way! I'm not doing that!" Iris expressed.

"Listen to me!" Lily snapped, in a no longer sweet tone, "go down there, and get Eliza...please."

Iris gulped in fear, then agreed to do it.

Iris crept into the room with the metal staircase and looked down to see what was down there.

She saw nothing but dim light and a greasy, cement floor.

She carefully went down and immediately saw Eliza's cell.

"Huh! You must be Eliza! I'm Iris, I'm here to get you out." But Eliza showed no excitement, or even care.

She was sitting on the floor of the cell, with her chin tucked into her knees.

"Hey! A human girl is up there waiting for you! You need to come with me!" Iris loudly whispered.

Again, Eliza showed no interest, instead ignoring the fairy.

"Alright, I don't know what's up with you, but I'm only getting free if you get free, so I'm getting you out of here."

Iris gripped the cell bars and started to tug.

"Aaarrrggghhh!"

Iris stopped, out of breath.

"Alright, time for plan B."

Iris took the dim light from the flame with her magic, and aimed it at the bars.

"I'll just melt 'em!"

She blasted the light at the bars, but the bars just absorbed the magic.

"What?" Iris exclaimed in confusion.

All of the sudden, Iris heard a *CLANG!*

"Hm?" She walked over to where she heard it, and saw a big metal key laying on the floor.

"Ahha!" She picked it up in delight and skipped to the cell.

Attentively, she turned the key, and the cell door opened.

"Yes! I did it!" But even though she was cheerful, Eliza was not.

Eliza hadn't moved, nor did she care.

"Oh, come on! You gotta work with me here!"

Iris walked over to Eliza and grabbed her arm, yanking it towards the door.

"Come on!" She urged, but still, Eliza did nothing.

Iris ended up dragging Eliza out of the cell, up the stairs and to Lily.

"What happened to her?" Lily asked.

"I don't know." Iris answered exhaustedly.

Lily picked Eliza up and laid her in her hands.

"Eliza?" Lily squeaked sweetly.

Eliza's eyes were fully open, but she seemed dead.

"Let's get her out of here."

"Wait," Iris demanded, "you have to let me go, because if you get caught, I'm in trouble too."

Lily nodded, "of course, you may go."

Iris smiled gratefully and flew away.

Lily got back to her crouched position, and headed back to where she came from.

Unfortunately, as Lily was walking through the foyer, a guard happened to be going through it too.

He called for backup, but before they could get there, Lily was darting for the forest.

She was out of the Palace and running in the direction of her horse, Casper.

The guards were close behind, slashing their swords at her back, but not reaching.

She ripped through the thick leaves and brush, following the sun that squinted through the narrow trees.

Once they made it far outside the main area, the guards were summoned back.

They instantly turned back for the Palace, and let Lily and Eliza go.

Even though the guards were no longer after her, Lily couldn't stop running. Her adrenaline kicked into full drive, and she ran the three miles back to Casper.

"Casper..." She mumbled when she saw her white horse munching on some leaves.

Her adrenaline ran out, and she tiredly got onto her horse's back.

"Come on Casper, let's go home..."

Five hours later, they made it to the stable and put Casper away so he could sleep. Then, they went to the secret garden.

Lily kneeled in the grass and poked Eliza awake.

Eliza sat up in Lily's palms, not wanting to look at her.

"Thank you, but I didn't need your help." Eliza said sourly, "I was fine in the cell."

Lily scoffed, "that's nonsense! Who's fine in a cell?!"

Eliza turned away and got on her feet, "well, I better be going, I have..ehe hem, a lot to do."

Lily looked down at her, "like what?"

"Just stuff! Ok?" Eliza replied sternly.

"Is this about Eliza? This isn't like you at all!" Lily tried to ask sweetly, but instead came out urgingly.

Eliza stared at the ground for a moment, then muttered "she's dead..." She tried not to cry, but the tears rushed through, "She was taken! She's gone!" Eliza sobbed.

Before Eliza could cry in front of Lily anymore, she left. She flew up into the sky, and flew until the wings on her back couldn't possibly support her anymore. She flew up the moon ruled sky, then until the sun took over with an army of colors.

Her wings became stiff, then she fell...

"Caw! Caw!"

Eliza woke up in a scratchy bed full of baby birds!

The mother was on her way, but before the mom could feed Eliza to her kids, Eliza got out.

Eliza's wings failed her when she tried to take flight, so she had to run.

The mother bird chased her, trying to peck at her.

"No! Leave me alone!" Eliza cried.

Eliza then ducked into the roots of a tree, and the mother bird thankfully got distracted by a worm wiggling around in fallen leaves.

Eliza's whole body was shaking fearfully, but once the mother bird left, Eliza crawled out of the crevice.

She gave an exhausted sigh, but the horror wasn't over yet.

A squirrel was climbing down the tree, right above Eliza.

"Aaahhhhh!" Eliza screamed.

The beady eyes stared at her, then curiously moved closer.

"Get away!" Eliza yelled while running.

The squirrel wasn't even chasing her, but Eliza didn't want to risk looking back. Then, a rabbit hopped out of its home, and also stared at Eliza.

"Aaahhhh!" Eliza screamed again.

Once the rabbit heard the scream, it hopped away, but they were by a pond, so dragonflies were near.

Eliza froze, listening to the buzzing, her heart stopped.

BUUUU ZZZ

The sound got louder...than louder...then...

BUUUU ZZZ!

"AAAHHHHH!!!" Eliza screeched.

She ran...She ran...She needed cover.

In the distance, she saw smoke.

A cottage! She thought.

She sprinted to the smoke, where there lay a cottage built between two trees.

The dragonfly was no longer after her, instead it went back to the pond.

Eliza darted to the cottage for shelter, but there were no openings where she could sneak in. No holes, no windows, no nothing– Just a door.

Eliza thought *how bad can it be? Maybe nice people live here...*

She knocked on the door with her tiny fist, and moments later a scary looking man opened.

He wore a black suit, with a black tie, and a white and navy striped trilby hat covering black, shaggy hair, but the most noticeable part about him were his eyes, his eyes glowed yellow.

"Yes...?" The man said in a questionable tone.

"um–oh–h–hi-I-I'm-uh, oh what's my name?" Eliza muttered.

"Hudson?" A voice from the cottage rang, "who's at the door, Hudson?"

Hudson snarled "just some fairy, who can't remember her name."

Eliza balled her fists.

"Well, bring her in, maybe she needs something."

Hudson fully opened the door, gesturing to Eliza to go inside.

Eliza gingerly stepped into the cottage.

The whole place was stacked with books upon books.

It wasn't a big place for a human, but to Eliza it was roomy.

The room had a yellow glow from the fireplace and candles. Some of the flames were dangerously close to the old books, but then again, it wasn't a big place, however there were A LOT of books.

"Hello..." A voice said from behind a pile of books.

"Um, hello." Eliza replied.

"So...are you looking for anything in particular?" The voice asked.

"Oh no, I just need shelter from the animals outside."

"Really? I don't recall there being anything too dangerous in these parts... What exactly are you hiding from?"

"Uh–a, um, dragonfly..."

"A dragonfly!?" The voice laughed, "why are you scared of a drag-onfly?"

Hudson interrupted, "Like I said, Sir, she's a fairy. They are very small."

"Oh yes, he did say that..."

Eliza nodded, even though the voice couldn't see her.

"Well isn't that something..." The voice added.

"You know, fairy...I could help you with that."

"Really?!" Eliza squeaked.

"Oh yes, I have many wonderful spells. I could make you the size of a human!"

"Wow! I would no longer have to run from birds!"

With that comment, Hudson let a chuckle slip.

Eliza glared at him, but that chuckle made up her mind.

"Could you do that for me?" She asked determinedly.

"Of course! Right this way."

Hudon gestured for Eliza to go toward the fireplace.

Once she did, she got a look at the body of the voice.

"Oh my!" She exclaimed.

"Yes, yes, I'm short!"

"No, I was just shocked because you're a wizard. I've never seen one before."

The wizard smiled and said "I like you, you're not cruel like those other people I've helped."

The wizard grabbed a glass tube filled with a pink liquid, then poured it into a glass tube filled with green liquid.

"Hudson! Get me the pig flesh glazed duckweed!"

"Right away." Hudson responded.

Hudson handed the wizard a deathly smelling, green goo, which he put in a cauldron along with the liquids.

The wizard stirred until smoke turned purple, then he poured the boiling sap into a tiny crystal cup.

"Here." He stated.

It smelled like rotten meat and algae.

"EW!" Eliza exclaimed after getting a whiff.

"This is the only way!"

"But it wreaks!"

Hudson grabbed her and forced her to drink the goo.

"BLEH!" Eliza gagged.

After a little bit of coughing, she started to feel weird.

Gradually, the pain and achy feeling increased.

Her limbs stretched and her abdomen widened, until everything stopped.

Now, she was looking down at the little wizard, but still slightly looking up at Hudson.

"I-It worked!" She shouted in excitement.

"Yes it did." The wizard responded.

Eliza jumped around and finally jumped in front of a mirror.

The picture in front of her startled her, making her fall over.

"Huuuh!" She gasped as she hit a pile of dusty books.

"Careful!" The wizard cried.

"W-W-what is that?!" Eliza exclaimed in horror.

"That's you!" The wizard replied.

Eliza was staring at an old, heavier-set woman, with baggy eyes and gray hair.

"No!" She cried, "That's not me!"

"Wait a minute..." The wizard said, looking around for something.

"It should be here somewhere.... Oh! Here it is!"

He picked up a long, pointy wand with vine shaped crystal looping around it.

"Here you go, hold this." The Wizard ordered.

Eliza heedfully clutched the wand, and was comforted as she held it. Her wand was unfortunatly taken she she was thrown into jail.

"That wand..." the Wizard explained, "That wand was gifted to me by an old friend—who was a fairy just like yourself. She had beautiful, elegant magic. So, her wand created beautiful, elegant spells.

The reason you looked hideous when my spell was casted to make you larger, is because magic reflects the heart. The spell will look however the intention took—thats a little rhym wizards use."

"Are you saying your intentions were ugly?" Eliza asked.

"no, no, no dear, my intentions were to help you. This is where is gets confusing. Spells that turn you into something your not, are usually intended to become forever deals. Forever deals are spells that make you a certain way forever. Since the intention was to make you last in this form for ages, you consequently aged..."

"Is there anyway to make me beautiful again? Or do I stay this way forever?"

"there are of course ways to make you lovely again, however the spells are as fleeting as youth. They only last so long."

"how do I do it?" Eliza asked curiously.

Eliza gently played with the wand in her hands, then realized the wizard was geaturing to the wand.

"The wand is quite beautiful, and if you transfer some of your magic into it, you may use it to make yourself beautiful."

Eliza looked over to him, "what's the limit?"

"Glad you asked. The limit is the time a spell has. Let's say you cast a spell, the spell will have a time limit depending on how strong the spell you cast is."

Eliza looked down at the wand, "hmmm, interesting."

Eliza tried to grab her fairy bag with her fingertips to get money for him, but before she could, she was already outside.

She looked up to find the cabin, but there was no cabin in sight.

What... Eliza thought to herself.

She looked around the forest, then up at the sky.

She tried to feel if she had wings, but she didn't feel them. She turned around in circles like a dog chasing its tail, but couldn't see any.

Huh! Do I not have wings anymore?

She frantically looked around, not knowing how to travel.

Then, she had an idea.

She waved her wand around and around over her head and said "bibbidi bobbidi boo!"

That just feels natural.

When she peeked her eyes open, she found herself in a garden. A garden filled with pumpkins and overgrown grass.

"Ahhh man, guess I need to work on that." She said to herself.

She made her way out, until she found a gorgeous home.

The backyard was almost as gorgeous as the house itself, but the backyard didn't even hold a candle to the front yard.

It was almost as if it was a small castle.

Eliza trudged through the yard and on the side of the house, to get to the woods. She was on her way into the woods, until she heard someone yelling from inside the house, "Oh Cinderella! My shoes need polishing and my dress needs sewing!" The voice was a high pitched, obnoxious squeal.

Another, more mature, voice responded, "Yes, step-sister!"

Hm. Eliza thought, shrugging her shoulders. She turned around to head into the woods, but then heard, "Cinderella! My bath is not drawn and my cat is not fed!" A meaner, angrier voice yelled from somewhere on the second floor of the house.

Cinderella must be a maid... Eliza thought.

"My apologies, I was cleaning up lunch and tidying Daria's room." The shy, beautiful voice responded.

"Did I ask for excuses?!" The cruel voice snapped.

"No, Stepmother."

Eiza stopped in her tracks. *Stepmother?*

Eliza had a quick flashback of Snow White's evil stepmother. Keeping Snow White in a tower, isolated from the world, and taking Beth captive, forcing her to use her magic for petty things.

Then she also remembered Lily complain about her stepmother. How her's never let her play and she always had to sneak out if she wanted to have any fun.

Eliza headed for the house, then peeked inside through the window.

The inside of the house was also magnificent, but what was happening inside was not.

Eliza heard water running, then moments later heard slight humming coming down the stairs.

Eliza turned her gaze towards the stairs, and saw a lovely, red-headed girl in a tatted dress prancing around, holding another dress. The dress she was holding was blue and covered in stitched flowers.

The girl held it up to her shoulders and twirled on the marble floors, humming a romantic song–but it all came to an end once she heard another shout, "Cinderella!" The girl abruptly froze and flung the dress over her arm. "Pick me some flowers from the garden! I'm trying a new look for the Ball!"

"Yes, step-sister!"

Cinderella galloped to the back door and into the garden.

Eliza watched her from the bushes.

"Hmmm hm! La LA La! Dadida!"

A couple of birds swarmed her while she sang, just like they did when Snow White sang.

"Well hello, Bluejay, and Robin. How are you today?"

The birds tweeted happily.

"Aawww, well I'm glad." Cinderella answered.

When Cinderella walked deeper into the garden, more animals came out to say hello, and she said hello back.

Cinderella indeed reminded Eliza of Snow White, the way they talked to animals, but their looks were completely opposite.

Snow White had pale skin and dark hair, with green eyes, while Cinderella had tanner skin, with blonde hair and blue eyes.

Cinderella gracefully picked flowers. She had roses, tulips, daisies and lilies.

Once she picked enough, she headed back to the house.

Eliza went back to her post at the window, and watched Cinderella walk up the steps and heard her open a door.

"Ugh, what took you so long?" asked a rude voice.

"I'm sorry, Anabelle..." Cinderella replied shyly.

Anabelle scoffed, then shut the door.

A few seconds later, Cinderella was back down the stairs, humming and dancing, until she saw the pink dress.

"Oh, how I wish I could attend the ball..." She commented to herself.

The ball? Eliza thought, *what ball?*

Eliza ran over to the house's front door. A nail was jammed inside with a bit of paper stuck to it.

Eliza touched the piece of paper with the wand and performed a recreation spell. A golden glow shone from the piece of paper and started to grow.

It spread until there was a long, glowing rectangle hanging from the nail.

The golden rectangle slowly became an ordinary piece of paper, with the Royal Ball's invitation printed on it.

THE RECEIVER OF THIS LETTER IS INVITED TO THE ROYAL BALL AT KING FRANCIS'S PALACE ON FEB. 15

Prince Charming is of age to receive his bride. The Kingdom is holding this Ball for him to choose a stunning lady whom he shall be wed. The Ball will begin at <u>8pm sharp</u> and last throughout the night.

Please be dressed accordingly.

So the Prince is to marry... Eliza thought out, *and Cinderella wants to go... Probably to show off to that Prince and maybe become his wife...*

Eliza tore off the recreated invitation and hid it in the bushes.

February 15th... That's in two days! Eliza realized.

Instead of going back to the window, Eliza decided to go into the woods.

Once she was out of sight, she began to practice her magic.

Blue sparks shot out of the crystal wand. They shattered into millions of pieces when they hit a tree trunk.

After about a second, the trunk began to twist and turn. The whole tree wrapped around itself before she could tell what was happening, and then, the tree finally stopped when it was in the shape of a dashing prince.

Oh my... Eliza thought to herself, *I never knew I could make such an intriquet sculpture...*

Eliza got very curious, and started blasting everything with her magic.

She finally got the hang of it when she learned she could turn plants and objects into ornate things.

However, when she finished, she realized that it was already midnight.

Oh my... she thought again.

She spent the next day deciding what Cinderella should call her.

Eliza is fine, She first thought, but then she noticed it wasn't making her feel powerful. She always heard stories of fairies using either their real names, or their color, but Eliza thought it would be uncreative to be called the Blue Fairy; which is the name of another fairy anyway...

How about... Nature Fairy! Once Eliza said it out loud, she ruled it out. It just didn't have the flare she was after.

Hmmmm... maybe it doesn't have to have a fairy in it...what about, Mysterious Lady!

No.

Tree Curver! Eliza the Elegant! Eliza Blue! Princess's Wish Giver! Cinderella's Hero! Blue Magic! ....The Fairy....

She was out of ideas.

Instead, she just decided to find a place to stay. Not wanting to sleep on those two longs again...

While she was looking around for an abandoned cabin or something, she realized that she could just create a home. A cozy hut made out of trees. It would be just like the one she made for her and Rose, however she was more powerful now and could make one that didn't look rotted out.

She stopped in her tracks and found a healthy looking willow tree.

She whipped her wand out and immediately shot a glistening, blue spark at the trunk.

Instantly, The trunk began to curve and twist. The branches looped around then dung into the ground. The trunk of the tree widened and became a cube. Holes started to appear and turn into squares. Two on each side of the entrance.

Lastly, the lance-shaped leaves of the tree covered the open top, and hung slightly about the doorway and windows.

Eliza walked up to the cabin and knocked on the wood; making sure it was more sturdy than the old one.

She has never seen a fairy that can do something like this! Even though she practiced and has seen what she can do, it still amazes her every time.

She twisted the yellow-shaded, amber doorknob, then proceeded to open the door.

The inside had plenty of space. Room for a bed next to the side window and even a closet.

The inside was completely wood, except for the leaves up above shielding the floor and whatever may be on it.

Eliza stepped over to the spot where she wanted her bed and shot another blast of magic. Promptly, roots from the tree dug up from the ground and through the floor. They spread out, then met each other in the middle.

After the actual bed was made, Eliza made sheets and blankets along with a pillow to place on the bed.

Once she was all done, she decided to go out and find food, but when she returned, it was already dark out.

"Where does the time go?" Eliza asked herself, looking up to the stars.

Eliza ate the berries she had collected, then fell into a deep sleep.

When she woke up, it was already 8:00 am, and she went back into the woods to find some breakfast.

Once she found a bush of blueberries and ate till her heart's content, she went to the house where Cinderella lived.

She went back to her post by the window. When she looked inside, she saw nobody, and she heard no voices.

Interesting... Eliza thought, *is nobody home?*

Just then, Eliza heard one of those obnoxious voices shout "Cinderella! My bed must be made and my bath must be drawn!"

Cinderella responded "but you usually don't take baths until dinner time..."

"Ugh!" The voice groaned, "Cinderella! I need the entire day to get ready! NOW DRAW MY BATH!"

"Of course, Anabelle! Right away!" Cinderella replied with a sincere tone.

Almost immediately, Cinderella appeared from a flight of stairs, probably leading to the basement.

She ran through the foye and up the stairs in a hurry to clean her step-sisters room and draw her bath.

Cinderella must have had to accomplish more tasks up there, because it took her five hours to return, but eventually, she came back and went straight down to the basement. Again, she was called to tend to someone's needs, "Cinderella! I need help with my hair!"

"Yes, Daria!"

Another hour goes by.

"Cinderella! I need help with my dress!"

"Yes, Anabelle!"

Half an hour goes by.

"Cinderella! Get my pearl necklace from my closet!"

"Yes, step-mother!"

Five minutes later Cinderella comes down to the foye huffing and puffing. She takes a short break in the middle of the floor, but then hurries back to the basement.

An hour later, a horse and carriage rolled up to the front of the house.

The coachman was dressed in a tuxedo and the horses were draped with white silk.

Once the coachman pulled up, Eliza heard the beating of high heels and the screeching of excited ladies, when they were scampering down the stairs shouting "coming my prince charming!"

Right before they were about to leave through the front door, Cinderella appeared from the basement in a beautiful blue dress, decorated with stitched flowers. The bottom rested on the floor and the straps slipped off the shoulders.

"Is there any room for me?" She asked shyly, but hopefully.

The woman stared at her in disgust, "absolutely not."

"But why?" Cinderella asked, frustrated, "I do all this work for you with nothing in return? Why?"

The step-mother shook her hand at Cinderella, and the two daughters took handfuls of mud.

Hesitantly, they spread it across the top and botton of her dress .

"HHUUHHH!" Cinderella gasped with tears in her eyes.

When they were done making a mess of her dress, Cinderella ran out sobbing.

She ran out to the backyard where the animals scrambled to comfort her.

She knelt down in the grass and cried into her hands.

Eliza followed her and watched the birds, squirrels and even mice look at each other, trying to figure out what to do.

That was Eliza's chance, but she had to make a big entrance.

Eliza whirled the wand above her head to magically teleport her infront of Cinderella. *Please work this time....*

Eliza appeared in front of Cinderella in a blue mist.

Huh, that's surprising....

"Dear girl... why are you crying?" Eliza asked. Of course she already knew the answer, but she didn't want to look like a stalker.

"*Sniff sniff*, I really want to go to the ball with my step-sisters and step-mother, but they ruined my dress and didn't let me go...*sniff sniff...*"

"Oh you poor girl, well, I can help you go to the ball." Eliza exclaimed with a mystical tone.

"*Sniff sniff*, really?" Cinderella asked hopefully.

"Of course! I can make you a dress and a carriage and…" She was saying while she was scanning the garden.

"Really?!" Cinderella exclaimed excitedly.

"Of course, my dear, I will make you the loveliest lady at that ball."

Cinderella stood up, and Eliza took that as her que to transform her into a princess. *I am really hoping my magic doesn't turn her ugly…*

She twirled her wand and felt a sense of goodness spread through her. Sparkles flew and Cinderella's stained dress magically turned into a blue, dazzled ball gown. Her hair became curled and made into a bun on top of her head. And as she twirled, Eliza noticed the spell gave her shoes that resembled the crystals on her wand.

"It's perfect!" Cinderella cried with joy.

"What do I call you?" Cinderella asked politely.

Eliza stopped and thought for a moment, then answered "Fairy Godmother…"

"Fairy Godmother?" Cinderella questioned, quizzing if it rolled off the tongue.

"yes…Fairy Godmother."

Because I'm not whatever evil step-mother she has.

Chapter Four

B eauty.... Love.... The one....

All of these were things Diana has heard before.

"You are beautiful!" One might say to her on the street.

"I love you!" Many men would half heartedly beg.

"You're the one!" a man once expressed.

How am I the one? Diana thought, *You've never even met me...*

Diana walked through her village and stopped at a small house, which was just stacked logs on top of each other, with holes carved into it, not even having glass covering them, just two sticks crossing each other.

She opened the poorly hung door and stepped into the one room house.

In the corner on her bed was one of Diana's little sisters, reading a brightly colored book.

"When will you throw that away, Ula?" Diana asked with a sigh.

"When I have read it for the thirtieth time." She responded seriously.

"Oh!" Ula gasped, "I have a letter for you, Diana! A boy came looking for you and asked if I could give it to you!"

Diana gave a disappointed sigh, then reluctantly read it, already knowing what it would say.

Dear Diana,

Your long, dark hair is as beautiful as the night sky that drifts me to sleep.

The bright blue eyes that pop out are the stars that guide wanderers home, and me to your charming presence....

There was more, but she crumpled it up and threw it with the others. The poetry that men tried so desperately to conjure up made her feel nauseated; kind of like some of the lines from her sister's book about princesses, princes, and happily ever afters....

"hey! You should love those letters! You're like one of these princesses!" Ula yelled while holding up her book.

Diana turned to her in disgust, "those princesses live in giant castles and have people waiting on them hand and foot! They have nothing better to do than read romantic letters all day."

"Humph."

Diana began to wash the dishes and put them away into the two cabinets that hung on three rusted nails.

Afterwards, she sat on her bed and layed down. She only meant to rest her eyes, but she ended up falling into a deep sleep...

Dressed in a long black dress with slit sleeves, covered in gold and jewels, she ran her kingdom.

"Forever reign, Queen Diana!" Thousands of people shouted against their will, repeatedly.

"Ugh!" Diana grunted, "the slaves aren't done with the garden yet!"

A man dressed in robes and jewels came up behind her and stated, "sorry, My Queen, you want such a big garden, but you gave them only little time to work on it..."

"UGH! Everyone is on THEIR side! Be gone!"

She swung her arm and he disappeared without a trace. After getting rid of him, she snapped her fingers and the garden instantly filled with black flowers.

She breathed in the smell of smoke with debris and.... *Loved it.*

"HHUUHH!" Diana gasped and jolted upward.

"Diana? Are you okay?" A tall boy with black hair asked.

"How long have I been asleep, Atlas?" Diana asked, holding her head.

"Um, about three hours."

"Three hours?!" Diana jumped out of her bed and ran out of the house.

She sprinted to the well to get water for dinner. When she reached it, she saw a crowd of people standing around it.

"What's going on?" Diana asked a lady standing at the edge of the crowd.

"The well is dry..." the woman stated, "it's the mermaids... They blocked up the river where the water comes from."

"But why would they do that?!"

"They said that they were done with our fisherman, taking all of the fish out of the ocean. So, to punish us they are blocking the river which runs through all of the wells."

Before Diana could throw in her opinion, the woman was called away by her husband; because he needed her to help him with the children.

Why is nobody doing anything about this? She angrily wondered to herself.

Instead of standing around waiting for water to come, she decided to have a little chat with the mermaids.

The village was close to the ocean, but also to a secret lagoon. The lagoon is hidden in a mile-long stretch of thick trees and overgrowth, but Diana and her brother, Atlas, found it when they were little kids. They were in trouble with mom and dad, so instead of getting punished, they ran away. Eventually, they found themselves deep in the same thick overgrowth, trying to find a way out., when suddenly, they found themselves at the lagoon's edge, peering down at the crystal clear water.

When mermaids showed up, they asked why they were there, so, they told them that they were lost. The mermaids were really nice about it, and helped them back by swimming them to their village's shore.

Mermaids were always so nice, so it was always hard to believe that they became so cruel to the village.

Diana made her way through the forest and after a miles walk, she finally found the lagoon. Once again, she was staring down at the crystal water, but even though the water was clear, you still couldn't see the bottom.

She waited a few minutes and two tails slapped the surface of the lagoon.

The tail on the left was a slimy green, and the tail on the right was a light purple. Under the now rippled water, two half human bodies were swimming underneath. Once they reached the lagoon's edge, their heads emerged. Taking in a deep breath of air and smoothing out their wet, slicked back hair, they turned to Diana.

"Hey human.... What are you doing here?" The mermaid with the light purple tail, along with caramel colored hair and green eyes asked.

"I–I uh–I am going to ask you to unblock the river. Please." Diana asked tensely.

"Unblock the river, huh?" The light purple mermaid mumbled.

"Hey, Sora," Interrupted the red tailed mermaid, "we should go..." The red tailed mermaid had vibrant, blonde hair. Although wet, it still shone like the yellow stars that sweep the night sky. The slight bit of sunlight that shone through the trees made her hair glisten even more. Even though she was the total resemblance of beauty, she was still quite shy.

"Why do you want to leave? We have to tell her the reason we blocked up that river!" Sora exclaimed.

"Bu–"

"Shush, Aris!— Look, Miss human, we didn't want to block up your river, but you gave us no choice. Stop fishing in our oceans and we will unblock that river!" She said in such a condescending tone it made Diana's skin crawl.

"But our village is known for our fish! That's how our village makes its money!" Diana pleaded.

"So find another way to make money! You humans are pretty good at that!"

Before Diana could strangle them with rage, they swam away.

"Aaarrrggghhh!" Diana yelled in frustration.

That night, she came back with no clean water from the well. Her three siblings were there waiting for her when she got back home.

Her two younger sisters, Morgan & Ula, and her older brother, Atlas.

"I'm so sorry, but there's no water— huh?" When Diana looked over, she saw a bucket of good, clean water, sitting by the kitchen table.

"Where did you get that?! All of the wells are dry!"

Morgan leaped up, "Alexander got it for us from his private well! Apparently, they have a well that collects underground water! So he gave us some."

"But why..." Diana asked, then when she asked, she immediately knew the answer.

She knew Alexander... He was from the wealthiest family in the village. He was a handsome young man, but had always thought money was the music of the heart.

Well.... Diana thought, *at least we have water...*

She began to boil the potatoes and use the extra water to wash the dishes from last night.

"Dinner time!" She excitedly called out to the one roomed house.

Everybody jumped up from their beds and sat around the wobbly table in the corner, by the window.

Everyone got their own potato and a handful of berries that Ula found in the bushes, growing beside their house.

In the middle of dinner, they got a knock on their door.

"I'll get it." Atlas offered.

"No, you keep eating, I think I know who it is..." Diana said.

When she opened the door, she found the same face she thought she would. She quickly stepped outside and dragged him to where her family couldn't hear.

"Hello, Alexander." Diana greeted.

"Hello, lovely Diana." He responded with dreamy eyes.

"Thank you for the water, I was able to cook–" She was stopped by Alexander's finger pressed against her lips.

"Shhhh, don't worry about it. Whatever you need, it's yours."

He lowered his finger off of her lips, but she was speechless. Not because she thought it was romantic, but because she thought he was so irritating!

He looked over at her house with a sad look.

"Poor thing..." He fake pouted.

Diana balled up her fist, ready to knock his perfectly straight, white teeth out... until he handed her a stack of money.

"Here. I'm not going to use it anyway."

Her fist turned into an open palm, and happily took the money.

She stared down at it, not sure if it was real, or a joke...

"I-I- I don't know wh–"

"Don't mention it." He exclaimed obnoxiously, with a swoosh of his perfectly groomed, blonde hair.

While Alexander was flaunting his "generosity", Diana was thinking...

Hmmm, so if I flash my pretty eyes at this clown, he gives me money?

"Oh, Alexander, I can't thank you enough." Diana exclaimed with her girliest voice.

"Like I said, don't mention it. It's just something I carry in my back pocket if I get hungry." He flipped his hair again.

I want to punch him so badly...

"Well, thank you, anyway. Would you like to join us for dinner?"

Please say no, please say no....

"I would love to!" He replied.

Reluctantly, Diana led him back to the house. When they arrived at the front door, Diana heard whispers in the house; obviously her siblings talking about them. When she opened the door, all went as silent as her parents' graves.

"Hello, everyone," Diana exclaimed, "is there any food left for my friend here?"

Diana gestured to Alexander, who was curiously scanning the room.

Her siblings quickly searched the table, looking for food they could give Alexander.

"Here!" Ula shouted when she noticed an apple by the window sill.

When Alexander looked at it, he frowned pathetically.

"Um, maybe we can share my meal." Diana pulled up a stool for Alexander to sit on, and then broke her potato in half.

"Here, you can have some of my berries too." She said as she scooped a bit of berries off her plate onto his.

"Thank you...." He grimly responded.

Alexander saw that there was no silverware on the table, but instead of saying something, he knew better not to.

After finishing his potato, he looked around the table at Diana's family. He looked at them, but they tried their best to look somewhere else.

Diana stood up and said "Alexander, it's getting late, I think it would be best to–"

CREEK!

"Ahhh! What was that?!" Alexander whined like a poor puppy.

"Oh," Morgan explained, "that's just our roof, it does that sometimes."

"I really think you should get that fixed." Alexander replied fearfully.

"Okay, Alexander, time to go."

When he stood up, the floor creaked too.

"Ah! You should get that fixed too! What happens when it breaks and you fall through?"

"It's fine, Alexander, it's done that for years."

"Then it's due!"

He gingerly stepped to the door and Diana opened it for him, but when she did, one of the hinges came loose and the top half of the door came undone.

"Ahhhh! That could have squished either of our toes!" Alexander shrieked.

His screams are more high pitched than Ula's...

Alexander cupped Diana's hands and said "you should come live with me. We have a guest house you could stay in. It's almost eight times the size of this one. My father and mother would be happy to have you live with us. You also don't ever have to do the dishes or clean or cook again, we have servants for that kind of thing." He looked up at her with big, round, glossy eyes, pleading for her to say yes to the proposal.

Diana looked around her house. The beds in the corner, the squeaking floor, wobbly table and the broken door.

This house is falling apart... She thought to herself.

Then she looked at her siblings. Their looks were as fragile as their future. With one decision, their lives could change forever.

But what's the better future?

"Alexander...." Diana started to say, but had to take one more look around.

"Yes!" Ula squealed.

"Ula!" Diana scolded.

"What?" She said, "we are living in a house that is near collapsing! Please Diana! Can we, can we?" She begged.

Alexander looked up to Diana hopefully.

"O-Ok."

"Yyyeeess—" Ula began to yell.

"No!" Atlas declared.

Everybody looked over at Atlas, dumbfounded.

"Alexander, do you mind going back home? We need to discuss this further as a family." Atlas said politely, but firmly.

Alexander nodded and sort of ran out of the house.

Atlas peered out the window to make sure he was gone.

"What the heck was that, Atlas?!" Diana exclaimed.

"What do you mean?" Atlas expressed, "you can't actually be thinking about moving in with that fool!"

Diana hesitated, "well... yes, I actually was."

"Why, Diana? You know he only wants you because you're beautiful. Once he proposes to you, and you say no, he'll kick you out on the street!"

"Well, what if I don't say no?!"

Atlas looked at her astonished, "you don't actually mean that...."

"Why can't I mean that, Atlas?! If I marry him then we can all have a better life. No more fixing the roof, or catching birds that swoop in from the window. No more going hungry, or thirsty, or moving around in your sleep and accidentally kicking your sibling! We would have our own rooms!"

"You know what, Diana? Fine, go ahead. Even though I'm your big brother, you seem to think you're the leader of this family. So, fine, if you and Ula want to live with him, then just go."

Diana grabbed her small amount of belongings, then took a little black box that was placed under her bed.

"Ula, are you coming or not?" Diana asked.

Ula looked around at her siblings, then up at the cracked ceiling.

"...coming." She mumbled sadly.

Alexander heard a knock at his door, when he opened, he saw the faces he was hoping to see.

"Diana!" He rejoiced, "welcome!"

He stepped out of the door and led them to the guest house. It was placed in front of their massive garden. They were growing tomatoes, strawberries, blueberries, raspberries, pumpkins and squash.

The house was definitely eight times the size of their old one. The door wasn't falling off its hinges and the windows had glass and shutters. The door knob actually twisted, instead of just hanging for decoration and some sense of security. There were several windows at the front of the house and at the sides. Flowers scattered all over the front porch and cute wooden railings, so you don't fall off the porch.

When they entered the house, Ula stood there, dumbfounded. There was an upstairs and the downstairs wasn't full of beds and kitchen ware.

"Wow!" Diana exclaimed, "what a lovely house!"

"Yeah... we built it a few years ago, sorry if it's dusty, the maid hasn't been here in a day." Alexander said as if it was a big deal. "Come, Let me show you where the rooms are."

He led them up the oak stairs to the second floor. Ula immediately went to the narrowest door and looked inside.

"Wow! This room is awesome!" She excitedly exclaimed.

Alexander chuckled, "that's the storage closet!"

"Storage closet?" Ula repeated with a puzzled look.

Alexander opened a larger door, and Ula rushed to go see inside.

There was a queen sized bed on the left side of the room, on top of white, carpeted floors. A huge window covered the wall ahead, looking out to the beautiful garden.

"Wwwooowww...." Ula expressed with wide eyes.

"So Ula, do you want this room?" Diana asked.

Ula nodded her head wildly.

"Well, then I guess this room is yours."

Alexander stepped over to the next door and opened it.

The walls were colored minty green and had the bed hanging from the ceiling in the center of the room.

Minty colored blankets were draped on the bed to match the walls and nearly twenty pillows laid perfectly neat on one side.

"This is gorgeous..." Diana said in awe.

"I'm glad you like it," Alexander expressed, "you even have your own bathroom."

He pointed to the right side of the room. An open entryway led to a white counter with a sink in the middle. To the right of the sink, a sliding door led to the toilet and shower/bath.

Amazing... Diana thought, *my looks have gotten me this far....*

"Do you like it?" Alexander asked hopefully.

"Of course I do. I love it." Diana smiled at him with her loveliest smile, and with that, he said "I can get the maid to cook you both dinner."

"Uh, we already had dinner." Ula commented.

"Oh, that? The potato and handful of berries? No, they'll cook you something real."

Before Alexander stepped out of the room, he gently caressed Diana's face. She smiled shyly on the outside, but on the inside she was thinking, *If only I didn't need you for your money.... You wouldn't have a hand anymore...*

While Alexander was out and the maids were cooking their dinner, Diana and Ula got a knock on their door.

Diana answered, expecting Alexander's parents, instead, she found her other younger sister, Morgan.

"What are you doing here?" Diana asked coldly.

"Can I live with you?" Morgan asked, almost brought to tears.

Diana widened the door, gesturing for her to come in.

About a half an hour later, the food came.

Grilled chicken along with mashed potatoes.

With no hesitation, they all dug in.

Even though there were only two meals, it was more than enough to share.

"Aahhhh," Ula exclaimed, "I am stuffed."

She collapsed on the bed and drifted to sleep.

Once she was snoring, Diana and Morgan got to talking.

"Why did you come here?" Diana asked.

Morgan hesitated, but then answered, "Atlas left. He left the house and I realized that was the first time I was home alone since..." She stopped.

There was a moment of silence, until Diana said "let's just go to sleep... It's been a long day."

Four months had already passed, and there was still no word from Atlas. Diana knew today was a big day, however, it was supposed to be a surprise. She made sure she wore her finest dress, and along with her finest dress, her finest jewelry. The maids had presented her with diamonds and rubies, but Diana had a specific necklace in mind for this important day.

She reached under her bed, where she stored her belongings from her old home. She took out a small, black box that her mother gave her before her passing. She cracked it open, and inside it was a beautiful, shell necklace. Her mother used to wear it for special occasions, which made it the perfect accessory for that day.

Alexander was down on one knee on a little white bridge. The sun was sinking down into the horizon and the waters were reflecting the colors that draped the nearly dark sky.

"Diana... Would you make me the happiest man in the Kingdom, and marry me?"

She peered down at the magnificent diamond that laid before her, pondering the future that it held.

"I will." She answered confidently.

Alexander jumped up with the ring and excitedly kissed her on the lips.

Everyone cheered as he slipped the ring onto her long, slim finger.

A week later, the wedding plans were going splendidly.

It would only be a few months before the big day, and Diana was already in anticipation for her new life to come.

"Oh, Diana, darling! It's time to measure you for your wedding dress!" Alexander's mother almost sang in excitement.

"Coming!" Diana replied, galloping down the stairs in a blush pink, satin dress.

"Oh, don't you just look stunning." Alexander's mother commented.

"Thank you, Vanessa, you're too kind."

Diana stepped onto a pedestal and a woman came up to her with a measuring tape.

"Hold still." She ordered Diana.

Vanessa sipped a glass of wine and asked "so, how many grandbabies will you and Alexander grant me?"

Diana was stiff for other reasons now.

"Um, I believe he said two children, a boy and a girl." Diana admitted.

Vanessa rolled her eyes, "Oh, I wish I got to choose. I wanted six children, one girl and five boys. I ended up with two children, both boys!" Vanessa chuckled at her own fate.

"I said hold still." The measuring lady hissed.

Once the dress measuring was finished, Diana and Morgan went to the flower shop.

The little bell rang when they opened the door. "Hello?" Diana said when she entered. From around the back corner, an elderly woman covered in daisies and tulips came prancing out to greet them.

"Hello! You must be Diana. And who is this lily that's made its way into my shop?" The woman asked playfully.

"Hi, I'm Morgan." she said in a sweet voice.

"Morgan, what a beautiful name! Now, here are all the flowers you ordered."

Suddenly, five men came around the back corner carrying as many flowers as they all could. Roses, orchids, carnations, peonies, liles and finally, lavender.

"Wow! I wasn't expecting all of this!" Diana expressed.

"We have a wagon you can borrow." The woman said.

Behind them, a man pulled a wagon up to the door, then the rest of the men carried the flowers to it.

Diana thanked them before she grabbed the wagons with Morgan.

They wheeled the wagon over the hill and through the roads. Everything was going fine until Morgan's wagon tipped over.

"Oh no!" They both yelled at the mess—but that wouldn't be the worst of their problems...

"WATCH OUT!"

BANG!

They jumped out of the way before the horse and carriage trampled them.

The carriage came to a screeching halt, after it hit the wagon and remaining flowers.

"I am so sorry, my horses didn't stop!" Said the horseman who jumped off the carriage to check on them.

Morgan was okay, because she jumped into the grass, but before Diana could get out of the way, her head was grazed by the fast moving carriage.

"My face feels bad." She groaned.

"My lady, I am so–" He reached his hand out to help her, but when he saw her face, he felt even worse.

"My lady..."

"What? What's wrong?" She asked worriedly.

The horseman rushed to get some medical supplies he carried with him.

He tried dabbing the bleeding from her cheek, but she shrieked in pain. "ahh! It hurts!" She cried.

Diana's face was horribly swollen and scratched.

"I need to see my face! I need to see my face!" Diana shouted.

The horseman than grabbed his bag and pulled out a hand mirror.

"No!" She yelled as she witnessed her face.

"Don't worry, Diana, it will probably look better in a few days." Morgan reassured her.

"*Sniff sniff*, no it won't! My face is broken!" Diana cried.

"Yeah, let's just get back to the house. We can bandage it there."

They snuck back to their house so Alexander wouldn't see them, then they rushed to the bathroom.

Morgan quickly got the bandages and wrapped Diana's face as well as she could.

Diana looked in the mirror and wanted to sob, but crying only caused her more agony.

"No!" Diana cried.

Morgan rubbed her back, "Don't worry, they will be healed before the wedding day. All will be fine."

"You don't understand! If my face isn't flawless then there won't be a wedding day!" Diana collapsed to her knees and began to sob.

"We should get you to a doctor." Morgan insisted.

"Okay.... but we can't let Alexander or his family see us."

Knock knock "hello? Diana, dear? Are you there?" Alexander called.

"Get the door, but don't tell him I'm here." Diana ordered Morgan.

Morgan went and answered the door.

"Oh, hello, Morgan. Is Diana there? I'm just wondering if you got the flowers."

Morgana looked down at the floor nervously.

"Well... We did have them... but we ran into some trouble..."

"Oh no! What kind of trouble?"

"Well... You see... Diana got hurt."

Alexander rushed into the house and Morgan directed him upstairs, to where Diana was sitting on the bathroom floor.

"Morgan, how could you!" Diana screamed.

"oh dear! We need to get you a doctor immediately!" Alexander yelled, while pulling Diana off the floor and darting outside.

They got to the doctor's office as fast as they could and got Diana examined.

"Well..." The doctor said after he examined her face.

"well, what?" Alexander asked nervously, "she'll be alright, right? Our wedding is in a few months, will her face be back to normal by then?"

"Well, I'm afraid I have some bad news...."

Everyone in the room held their breath.

"Her face is so severely fractured, that her face may never look the same again."

The breath that Diana held in got knocked out of her.

"Where are we going to go?" Ula asked sadly.

"You two are going to go stay with aunt Audrey in Northern Town." Diana answered.

"Where are you going to go?" The two younger sisters asked.

Diana hesitated, "none of your concern."

"What?" Morgan scoffed, "why can't you just come with us?"

"I just can't!" Diana shouted.

Why is this forest so big? Diana asked herself in exhaustion.

She had been wandering the forest for two days, endlessly searching for something.

Again, nightfall hit.

Time to go sleep under a tree again...

Diana found herself a wide trunk to rest her back on. Before she fell asleep, she heard rattling in the bushes.

Probably just rabbits again... She thought calmly to herself.

When she was about to fall asleep, again, she heard more rustling. The rustling got louder and louder, then closer and closer.

Diana kept her eyes on the suspicious bushes, waiting for a little bunny to jump out.

Instead, a tall, dark figure arose from the brush.

"AAHHH!" Diana screamed in horror.

The tall, dark figure vanished into the darkness, and Diana no longer felt at peace.

She stood up and started scanning the forest for the figure.

There were no more shadows and no traces of anything that could have been from it.

Suddenly, she heard something behind her.

Fearfully, she turned around.

"AAAHHH!"

"Where am I?" Diana panicked.

Her back was pressed up against a wall and all she saw ahead of her were piles of books.

When she turned her head, she saw a tall man leaning up against the wall, sleeping.

He was wearing a black suit and tie, with a matching black fedora.

His hair was messed up underneath the hat, and he snored as though he was almost growling.

When Diana attempted to stand up, the man's eyes popped open.

"AH!" Diana yelled and stumbled backwards.

The man turned to face her, and she saw that his eyes were glowing yellow.

"W-Wh-what are you?" Diana asked.

The man didn't answer, instead he turned away.

Out of nowhere, she heard a mysterious voice say, "Oh Hudson, don't be rude."

Immediately, Hudson straightened his back at attention.

The voice spoke again, "come here, girl, we need to talk."

Hudson gestured for her to follow him through the stacks of books.

Hesitantly, Diana followed him.

Once she passed the fourth book pile, she saw the small man.

He was crouched on the floor, reading a very thick book, with several other books near him.

The little man had a long white beard, and wore a blue robe.

Despite his size, Hudson seemed very scared of him.

Before Diana got her chance to speak, the little white bearded man spoke first.

"A vain heart is always cold." He said in a somber tone.

"Excuse me?" Diana asked, confused.

For the first time, the little man looked up at her.

"Who knew beauty could be so dangerous?"

Diana scoffed, "So what are you supposed to be? A dwarf?"

The little man ignored her crude remark.

He closed the book he was reading, and blew out the candle.

That small section of the hut was dark, but not for long.

Diana was scanning the dark, until a green light glowed.

The little man was pouring liquids into a cauldron, making it glow and bubble.

While he was throwing items into the mysterious mixture, he called out funky words that Diana had never heard before.

BAM! A cloud of green smoke filled the entire hut. Diana started coughing, but it suspiciously didn't affect Hudson at all.

Once the smoke cleared, the little man poured the green liquid into a vile.

He walked over to Diana with a very serious look on his face.

"W-what are you doing with that?" Diana asked, startled.

The little man stuck out his hand, but Diana didn't understand.

Before she decided what her move was, he was holding her necklace.

Without thinking, Diana tried grabbing it. "Give it!" She demanded.

The little man dodged her hand and stepped back, "I will not make the same mistake I did so many years back!"

Diana put all of her weight into that grab, so she fell forward into a pile of books. Before she could get up, the little man already poured the liquid into her shell necklace.

"What did you just do?" Diana shrieked.

The shell on the necklace started to glow a golden color. After a few seconds, it dimmed down until it was back to normal.

The little man stared down at the necklace, "Hudson…"

In the blink of an eye, Hudson's arms were under Diana's, holding her in place. Diana struggled ferociously, but he didn't budge.

Before she could try to escape again, the necklace was around her throat.

"AAHHH!" She shrieked as though she was in agony.

Hudson let go of her, and she fell to the floor, screaming.

The little man stared down at her, out of breath. "Good, now without your beauty, innocent lives will be spared."

Diana stopped screaming, and scowled up at him, "what do you mean, without my beauty?" she growled, "do you see my face?! It's already gone!"

The wizard rolled his eyes, "any wizard, witch or fairy could have fixed that. However, my intent was to imprison you with my power. Now you will be as ugly as a fish in the depths of the sea.

"My name is Bartholomew, and I am one of the first Wizards. I have given you part of my power, so you will forever be bound to the misery and isolation of this curse."

Diana's grip loosened on the necklace, "wait a minute… I read about you in a book I was given by my sister. How in the world do you think giving me power will make me weaker? You fool, you've only given me what I've been looking for all along!"

Wizard Bartholomew paused for a moment, "you don't understand yet, but this way, you are only capable of half the destruction you would have caused... Because now your outward appearance will be as ugly as your soul."

Diana's hand left her necklace and plummeted to the floor. She began to stand up, but before she could, Wizard Bartholomew snapped his fingers.

Uuuggghhh, where am I? Diana thought to herself. She saw the chambers of air float above her head and then disappear into an abyss of darkness.

She looked around and spotted colorful coral and a few fish. On instinct, she began to hold her breath, then realized she could breathe just fine.

Interesting... Diana thought. She tried to swim like she did as a kid, but she was struggling.

She looked down at her body, but it wasn't what she remembered.

Her stomach bulged out and her feet were no longer feet.... They were coiled tentacles.

"AAAHHHH!" Diana screamed.

Once she figured out how to move, she began searching for a shelter.

After a while of searching, she found a dark cave.

Without hesitation, she swam in. Once she got a little deeper into the cave, seaweed started glowing, giving minimum light.

A few yards deeper, she found a wide room, illuminated with glowing seaweed.

Excellent... She thought as she scanned the space.

As she passed, the seaweed would glow brighter. The entire cave as lit and something in the corner caught her eye. It was large, reflective stone. When Diana peered at it, she was eye to eye with a monster.

Thin, grey lips with scaly, green skin. Hair that coiled like the tentacles that replaced the feet and legs, along with wrinkled, sharp fingers that had no nail beds at all. Once she realized that was her, her heart became darker than the corners of the cave that were never illuminated.

So there is a new Mermaid King, hm? Diana thought as she swam around her cave.

"There will be a ceremony crowning the king and his wife. I want to go, maybe bring a present..." She said to herself with an evil laugh.

Diana swam over to her coral cauldron and grabbed a vile filled with fairy powder.

She sprinkled a pinch of the golden dust into the bubbling liquid. *Too bad that wizard didn't restrict beauty spells!*

The cauldron started to smoke and rumble.

"HAHAHA!" Diana screeched, as she disappeared into a cloud of magic smoke.

After a long trip, Diana finally made her way into the Mermaid Kingdom.

Before she reached the city, she hid behind enormous coral.

She popped open her magical liquid and drank it.

After a few moments, her skin began to stretch.

"AAHHH!" She yelled.

Eh, I didn't expect it to hurt this bad.

"AH!" She yelled again in pain. Her tentacles came together and her face stretched tightly. Her hair began growing rapidly and it seemed as though her weight was falling off.

Fortunately, the pain only lasted for a few minutes.

When she looked at herself, she almost cried.

Her face and hair were back to normal and instead of legs or tentacles, she had one beautiful tail that matched the color of her black hair.

"WWEEE!" She celebrated as she swam in quick circles.

"Ah! I feel alive!" She cheered.

Before Diana got too carried away, she reminded herself of the spell limit.

Yes, I am only like this until midnight....

Diana didn't waste any time getting to the palace.

When she arrived, she saw that every possible entry way was well guarded.

At the main gate, every mermaid was checking in.

Shoot, you need an invitation! Diana acknowledged worriedly.

She looked up at the other entry ways, but they were all guarded, how was she going to get into the palace?

AH HA!

A large group of mermen and mermaids were rushing in through the main entrance. The party had already started and they were late.

Diana quickly and discretly snuck into the middle of the crowd. The guards were so overwhelmed by the herd, that they were only able to check a few invitations before they had made it into the palace.

I made it!....

She found a seat near the back, and just waited in anticipation of who the new King would be.

All of the sudden, a voice filled the room, "please stand."

In union, everybody stood.

"We are here today to witness the crowning of the new King. This is a special day indeed, for never before has there been a king not of royal blood."

A seriousness fell over everybody.

The King isn't of royal blood? Well this is interesting...

"We welcome the lovely Queen Aris, who is of royal blood, to crown her husband."

The giant doors opened and all was silent in anticipation.

Suddenly, a gorgeous mermaid with long, blonde hair and a red tail made her way to the stage.

I know her... Diana recalled. She had a flashback of the secret lagoon, where the mermaids would hang out. She remembered Aris, being shy and scared of her; since Diana was a human back then.

But now, Aris was confident. She appeared before everyone, staring assertively at the door ahead of her, with a golden crown in her hands.

"Presenting!"

Everyone froze.

"... Sir Atlas!"

what?...

A masculine looking man emerged from the doors. He had a long, green tail and dark hair. His cheeks and jaw were chiseled, but smooth. His eyes were wide, but always narrow.

No doubt, that's MY Atlas!

He swam to the stage and faced the crowd.

A mermaid in front of Diana commented, "oh, he's so handsome."

Diana made a disgusted face.

"Please be seated!" The voice announced.

In union, everybody sat down.

"This is the crowning of Sir Atlas! A true, noble merman!"

Merman? Last time I saw him he was just a frustrating little boy...

"Let the crowning, commence!"

Atlas kneeled, and Aris hovered the golden crown over his head.

After a few moments, she carefully set the crown on his wavy, dark hair.

Instantly, everyone shouted, "King Atlas!"

Atlas rose and turned his back to the crowd.

Aris went near the back and uncovered something called the trident. It is a huge golden fork that gives the wielder control over the sea.

Once it was uncovered, Aris quickly hurried away from it.

Atlas confidently went over to it, and placed his hands on it.

A golden flash darted through the water, and rattled the entire palace.

Atlas squeezed the trident and then lifted it up. The whole crowd was in awe, even Diana, but she didn't know why...

"Long reign King Atlas!"

At the after party, all of the kingdom was invited. They all danced, ate and celebrated, but there was one who didn't...

Diana kept herself in the corner of it all, grimly staring at her brother; the king, the whole time.

Once four and a half hours was stripped away, Diana knew she only had fifteen minutes remaining.

"Hold this." Diana commanded the mermaid sitting next to her, tossing her a shrimp tail.

Diana made her way over to Atlas.

"Atlas! How are you? I can't believe you're married!" She said sarcastically with a hint of amusement.

"Uh–" Atlas squeaked out when he saw Diana's face.

"Oh, look! He's speechless, isn't that cute?" Diana chuckled to Aris; who was beside Atlas.

"Uh– I'm sorry, who are you?" Aris asked Diana.

"Oh me?" Diana responded dramatically.

"She– She's no one you have to worry about, dear." Atlas exclaimed, trying to cover up Diana's existence.

Well that stung...

"Oh, of course, I'm no one important, just his sister!"

"You have a sister?..."

"Well, yes, but–"

Diana faked a shocked gasp, "you never cared enough about me to mention me?"

"That is not tru– ehem, sorry about all of this, Aris... I just didn't expect her to be here, that's all."

Atlas looked down at the sea floor, ashamed.

"Atlas..." Aris said sympathetically, "you are my husband... But more importantly the King of Seas. You do not have to explain yourself to me."

Their foreheads connected passionately, and Atlas expressed "you, my dear, are the most important thing..."

"Cringe!" Diana shouted through the party, "Hey Atlas, since Aris is the most important thing, hand it over!"

Smoke surrounded Diana and she grew into the monster that consumed her. Once she was back to her scaly form, she tried to grab the trident.

Reflexively, Atlas pulled away.

Once Diana's swat missed, one of her tentacles snatched Aris.

"Aris!" Atlas shouted, "give her back!"

"You know what Atlas? I guess you will have to choose which is more important. Your power, or your family..." Diana snarled.

"AAAHHH!" Atlas yelled as he held the golden trident up to the waters.

Gold shimmered from the trident and blinded Diana for a moment. Before she could gain back her sight, she was thrusted away from the waters, being forced to let Aris go.

Diana was then forth banished from the Kingdom, never to return again.

"How dare he! How dare he!" Diana proclaimed through her cave.

"He left us! He ditched Morgan! To become a..a.. Fish king!"

She threw a cup with such force it shattered one of her jars.

"I must destroy him! I must destroy him entirely!"

But how?... She thought, *he has that stupid trident...*

A few weeks later, Queen Aris announced that she was pregnant with triplets.

Once Diana heard the exciting news, she got an idea.

Of course... No need to take away his power... Just take away his loved ones...

Diana chuckled at the ingenious plan that sparked into her brain.

Nine months after the news of the triplets, they were born.

The Queen and King named them Ava, Anna, and Adele.

Diana collected as much information about the girls as she could, so maybe one of them could fit the plan.

Unfortunately, for Diana, there wasn't much information she could gain from an infant, but she was prepared for that.

Two years later, Diana found out none of them would be suitable.

Ava, the oldest, had ginger hair and a ginger tail to match. She was obviously pretty, but she had no extraordinary gifts.

Anna, the second child, had dark hair like Atlas', with a purple tail. She reminded Diana of Ula, so much so, that that is the reason Diana couldn't use her.

Adele, the third child, had plain brown hair with a blue tail. Though beautiful, her voice was squeaky and unappealing.

Diana was now doubting her plan, but she learned that the King and Queen were pregnant again, with twins.

Nine months later, the twins were born. Thankfully, they were both mermaids.

Another two years passed, but Diana still didn't get "the one".

Aris; named after the Queen, the fourth daughter, seemed promising at first. She had wavy blonde hair and bright blue eyes, with a red tail. She was lovely, but had a sassy and rude attitude.

Her younger twin, Amara, had plain brown hair with an ugly brown colored tail.

"It's useless!" Diana shouted as she punched the cave wall. "They have had five children, all mermaids, and none of them have been good enough!"

Just as Diana was about to give up, she heard that the King and Queen were expecting again!

"Yes!" Diana cheered, "another chance!"

Nine months later, The Queen gave birth to a single baby mermaid.

Again, Diana waited until the child was older, but in only one year, the Queen was pregnant again!

Andrea was the sixth daughter's name, but Ursula could already tell in one year that Andrea was not it.

Nothing was wrong with her appearance, she had blonde hair and a pretty violet tail, but she was just too shy.

"That's it! They will never raise a daughter that is suitable!"

Ursula gave up on the entire plan, and came up with a new one.

Not as clever, but clever enough to destroy the King.

Sadly, for Diana, all of her plans took very long to happen.

This one in particular took five years...

Diana first had to wait until Queen Aris was done having children, which was after her seventh child.

Then, she had to wait until the children were old enough not to need their mother around all the time, which took about three years.

Diana somehow had to track Queen Aris everywhere she went outside of the Kingdom.

Diana wanted to make sure that Queen Aris still visited that lagoon.

After another year, the Queen felt comfortable to travel back to that lagoon, and started to visit regularly.

Once Diana knew this, she cast a spell that would only last for an hour; because she was saving her power. She gave herself feet.

She returned to being human and tried to convince everyone in her old village that the mermaids were enemies.

To do that, she dried up the well again.

"It's the mermaids!" Diana cried.

She tried and tried before her time was up, but the people were so stubborn that they would never hurt a mermaid.

Diana had to wait until she could cast the spell again, which usually lasted a month.

Each time, Diana would do something to the village and try to convince the villagers that it was the mermaids, but always, it would never be enough.

She needed something that would really provoke the villagers. Something that told them that they were at war with Sea Kingdom.

The village was known for their fish market. That's how the village made most of its money. So, what if a mysterious incident happened to their fishing boats? Maybe something that they knew only mermaids could be behind?

Diana went back to her cave and started casting a spell.

Instead of smoke, powerful whirlpools formed.

They made their way to the fishing grounds, and sunk every last one of the boats.

Diana was too weak to turn herself into a human, but the villagers didn't even need a push.

"The mermaids! They did this!" People shouted.

"Yeah! They've been wanting to get rid of us for years!"

"Now is our chance! Lets get 'em!"

A herd of people jumped on their still in tacked boats with nets and spears.

Diana began to think, *they will destroy themselves...*

However, before the villagers could make it out of the bay, a mermaid appeared in distress.

"What do you all mean? Why would you blame us for this? We did nothi–"

Queen Aris was caught with the net and hoisted onto the boat.

"No more lies!" The men shouted.

"No more Queen Aris! The mermaids will know our wrath!"

They sailed back to shore and took the Queen with them...

Hurricanes churned across all of the seven oceans.

Waves were fifty feet high, circling the Pacific.

"Humans will feel my wrath!" Atlas roared through the sea.

He swatted his trident back and forth, causing tsunamis.

"Excuse me... Your Majesty?" Atlas' advisor asked nervously.

Atlas ignored him with his murderous rage.

"I-If you keep doing this... You will destroy humanity..." The advisor told him.

"Good! They will pay!" The trident glowed a violent gold. The waters shook around its fury.

"Stop!" The best friend of Queen Aris shouted, "it wasn't all humanity! It was just that stupid village!"

The thrashing stopped and he glared at her with a blank, blood thirsty stare.

"Which village..." He growled.

The mermaid started to shake. "Um, uh, I-"

"Which village!" He yelled angrily.

"The east village!" She yelled fearfully, "the east village in the Rose Kingdom!"

Without hesitation, Atlas whirled the trident around. The fierce glow gave off a paralyzing feeling.

The burst of power came out like a bullet, and quickly made its way to the unexpecting village, leveling it to the ground.

Once Atlas knew the village was gone, his rage turned to depression.

He fell to the floor and began to weep.

His daughters were taken away from the site by the guards.

"Yes!" Diana cheered in her cave when she heard the news.

"It worked! It worked! The King is broken!"

She danced around the cave and wretched souls she's collected over the years.

Every day after that, Diana turned her cave into a business.

She took in needing customers and granted their wishes, for a price.

She did this for years, feeling like she conquered the ocean, she even picked up a well known title as The Sea Witch.

Except, after years of healing, Atlas once again ruled the ocean.

"No!" Diana cried, "it wasn't enough! He came back!"

"I must destroy him again..."

She thought about how, but she couldn't think of anything good enough. Except for one idea, her earlier idea.

But there are no suitable daughters for the plan... She thought.

While she was pondering, she remembered a daughter that she never learned about.

"Of course... the youngest... I never bothered to learn her name, did I?"..... I guess I'll just call her Little Mermaid."

Little Mermaid had astonishing golden hair, like her mother, and a green tail too. From what Ursula gathered, she found out Little Mermaid had a lovely personality, and the most amazing singing voice.

It was said that she could freeze the audience with one note.

Perfect...

Diana just had to think of how to lure Little Mermaid into the trap.

While she was thinking, she remembered a client that needed to change from a crab into a seahorse to be with the one they loved.

Then also, she remembered that Atlas turned from a human into a mermaid to be with Aris.

"I just need Little Mermaid to fall in love with the prince of the Rose Kingdom! That plan is perfect! I just need to get her interested in the human world!"

Diana would frequently lay items from the human world on the sea floor, for Little Mermaid to find. Luckily, Little Mermaid took interest and would store the items away.

Diana waited a few weeks until a ship cruised the waters with the Prince of The Rose Kingdom aboard.

She cast a simple spell that made the waters underneath the ship get violent—violent enough to crash it.

Luckily, Little Mermaid found it and saved whoever she could, including the handsome prince.

Gazing into his unconscious face, she already felt love.

Excellent... Diana cheered, *this plan is working better than I could have wished for...*

All Diana had to do was wait...

She sent some of her enslaved souls to convince the little mermaid to visit The Sea Witch.

Ursula sensed her presence from miles away.

The mermaid entered the cave gingerly. Looking around curiously and hesitantly.

"I'm right here, dear." Diana said welcomingly.

The mermaid swam up to her, cautiously.

Diana decided not to comment on her nervous behavior, instead she got right to the point.

"You want to be with that human boy, correct?"

The little mermaid looked at her funny, "how do you know about that?"

"I know everything, sweet child." Diana replied. "I don't blame you... He is quite a catch." Diana continued, "but to be with him, you must be a human yourself."

"Well, I understand that, but can you really do that?" She asked hopefully.

"Oh honey! I can do anything!" Diana responded excitedly.

"I grant unfortunate creatures their desires.... For a price, of course."

The mermaid thought about that for a moment, "what kind of price?"

"Well..." Diana started, "it's less of a price, and more of a deal."

She looked at her with a puzzled face.

"For your wish, I will make you a spell that will turn you into a human for three days. However, within those three days, you must receive a true love's kiss from the Prince. If you do, then you will remain a human, but if you don't, then you become my slave. Simple.." Diana explained.

The mermaid pondered what would happen if she remained human.

"I would never see my father or sisters again..." She admitted.

"But..." Diana added, "you'll have the prince..."

She pondered this for a few moments, then agreed.

"Excellent!" Diana shouted, trying to contain her excitement.

"But there is one more thing... payment." Diana added.

"But I already made the soul deal with you..." She exclaimed.

"Yes, but what happens when the prince falls in love with you? Then I would do all that work for nothing..."

"Oh... That makes sense... How much will this cost?"

Diana scoffed, "It's not money, dear, it's your voice..."

"My voice?!"

"Yes, your voice. No more singing, talking, humming—"

"But without my voice, how can I–"

"You'll have your looks!" Diana interrupted bitterly, "don't forget the importance of a pretty face, deary. " Diana chuckled, remembering Alexander.

"Is that really all I need?" The mermaid asked unsure.

Diana scoffed once more, "trust me, sweetie, it's all a man wants."

When Diana said this, she made a picture of the Prince appear before the mermaid, convincing her to make the choice.

When she looked at him, her expression was in awe.

I got her... Diana acknowledged to herself.

She snapped her fingers and made a golden scroll appear. She handed her a writing tool and said, "just sign your name..."

Partially reluctant, she signed her name quickly on the bottom of the contract. Not like Diana would truly need it, but more for the purpose of making the mermaid think she made a real deal.

Immediately, The Sea Witch began to brew her spell. While she was brewing, the mermaid was forced to sing and her voice left with every note. Entering the glowing shell necklace around Diana's neck.

Once everything stopped, the mermaid was mute, but also on the beach with legs...

"We got her! My plan worked like a charm!" Diana cheered.

"Now... time to ruin that girl's life... and make mine unstoppable."

Diana raised her fist into the water, "you hear that wizard! There is a flaw in your plan after all!" Diana brutally laughed.

One day in, Diana transformed herself back to her stunning, human self. She had only one intention in mind, and that was to make the Prince her own.

"Um, Mistress? May I ask what your plan is?" One of the souls asked nervously.

"My plan?" Diana responded, trying to clarify.

"Yes, your plan... Is it just to take that little mermaid's soul?"

"Oh no, it is much more than that... You see, I was cursed to be an ugly sea creature, however, I learned how to control the power the wizard gave me through this necklace. I am not able to break his curse, but I'm able to cover it up. Understand this, to cast a transformation spell, I need to have an object of beauty. However, nobody ever said it needed to be a PHYSICAL object. I found a loop hole! Beauty is fleeting, but voices aren't! You may not have your smooth skin forever, but your voice is a different story. Her voice was the impression of beauty that doesn't cease! MY LOOKS WILL NEVER DIE!"

"I want to destroy my brother, King Atlas. And to do that, I must take away the things most precious to him... his family. So, that's *part* of the plan... The other part is the sneaky part. While that mermaid is desperately trying to make the prince fall in love with her, without being able to speak, I will come in with my beauty and stunning voice to make him mine... And once I wield the power of a kingdom, I will rule the world!"

The soul asked, "But I thought your spells had time limits? So, once he figures out you're a monster, he won't love you anymore..."

"I just told you! As long as I have the voice to concentrate my power, my looks will never fade!"

The soul pondered this for a moment, then just shrugged.

On the second day of the mermaid's aspiration, she heard a beautiful voice coming from outside her room on the beach.

When she peered out, she saw that there was a gorgeous woman singing.

She was enjoying the melody, until she saw a man approaching the woman.

My prince! She acknowledged in shock.

the Prince approached Diana curiously.

Diana was ready for the Prince to bow at her feet and worship her, but that never came.

"Sorry ma'am, but this is a private beach." The Prince stated, not at all in awe of her beauty.

"What?" Diana responded in shock.

"This is a private beach." The prince repeated, "and I have a lovely lady sleeping near here, so I'm asking you to leave."

Diana just stared at him, dumbfounded.

When the Prince gestured the way out, Diana lost it.

"You jerk!" She yelled.

"Hhhaaaahhhhhaaaaaha!" Diana started singing, "hhhhaaaah-hhhhaaaahhaaa!"

While the song continued, the Prince's eyes became dimmer and dimmer. Until the song ended, and he was completely empty.

The mermaid was watching all of this happen from her bedroom window. Not being able to hear what they were saying. All she saw was them communicating, and then the Prince held her hand!

Diana took control over the Prince, casting a spell over him, making him into her slave.

"Come now, my prince, we must tell everyone of our engagement." Diana ordered.

The Prince took her hand and walked with her, agreeing with everything she said.

My destiny has led me to this... I will be all powerful!

Chapter Five

An illness spread across the village, but no cure was ever found until years later.

"Mother! Father!" Atlas cried out, as he was lying beside them.

"I'm sorry, son..." His father said as the light dimmed in his eyes.

His mother put her weak hand on his face and said "tell your siblings that I love them..." Her hand dropped, and Atlas began to mourn.

When Diana, Morgan, and Ula came home, every grocery in their hands dropped. They ran to their parents and grieved.

Two days later, they had a lovely funeral for their parents.

Friends showed up, the flowers were radiant, the pastor's words were soothing and hopeful, but by the end, not one of the children stayed.

Diana went off into the forest.

Atlas followed.

Morgan headed home.

And Ula went to a friend's house.

They all handled their grieving differently, but none of them took it well, especially the oldest two...

"Diana! Where are you going?!" He yelled as he tried to follow her.

She never replied, instead, found a way to lose him.

Atlas looked around, but he couldn't see Diana anywhere.

Where did she go? He wondered to himself.

As he scanned his surroundings, he realized he had been in these woods before. When him and Diana were children, they ran away from home to avoid the consequences of some dumb mistake, and found themselves lost with no trail to follow. Eventually, they found a small lagoon with two mermaids that helped lead them back home.

Atlas had traveled too far into the woods to know where his village was, but he might know where to find the lagoon.

Where is it?! He thought to himself. He had been searching for hours, but all of the forest looked the same, he had no idea where he was.

Before he took another step deeper into the forest, a voice rang out.

It was a singing voice.

It was soothing and lovely. Atlas had never heard a voice like that before.

He followed it, hoping to find civilization. Instead, he found the lagoon, with a beautiful mermaid inside, singing the enchanting melody.

"Oh!" The mermaid gasped when she realized Atlas was watching.

"You scared me." She giggled nervously.

"Oh, don't be scared, I don't mean any harm." Atlas told her.

The mermaid still backed away cautiously.

"I-I'm Atlas... what's your name?"

"uh-um..I'm–my name is Aris."

"Aris... That's a beautiful name." Atlas said in awe of her gorgeous name and beauty.

Once they exchanged names, Aris was more comfortable, but still cautious.

"Anyway," Atlas said, "I'm a little–Um, lost."

They stared at each other for a few seconds, until Aris started to giggle. Her giggle was sweet and gentle, but a little amused.

"You're lost?" She asked.

"Yeah," Atlas responded, "could you maybe show me the way back to my village?"

Aris slid off the ledge where she sat, and swam up to Atlas.

She looked up at him with a passionate gaze. She held her hand up to him, for him to take her hand.

Once he did, she carefully led him into the water.

Without any questions, Atlas followed her.

Aris quickly swam them through the underwater passageway.

She made sure to keep Atlas' head above water, until they made it back to his village's shore.

Aris stayed in deep water, and Atlas swam the rest of the way to the beach.

When Atlas made it, he immediately looked back for Aris; who was still watching him.

He waved at her, to say goodbye, and she waved back, only in a longing way.

Atlas kept his eyes on her, but she ended up swimming away.

Atlas made his way back to the house, and found Morgan on her bed.

Neither of them said anything the rest of the day, as they waited for Diana to come back.

Once she did, they still said nothing to each other the rest of the night.

About two years passed. They were all waiting for Diana to get back with the water to boil the potatoes, but hours passed and she still wasn't home.

"Where's Diana?" Ula asked Atlas worriedly.

"She should be here soon." Atlas said hopefully.

Right after he said that, there was a knock on the door.

When Atlas opened it, a little lady in a maids outfit was carrying a large, heavy bucket of water.

Atlas gestured to her to come in.

She set the bucket of water on the table, and sighed in exhaustion.

After a few breaths, she froze in an upright position.

"Hello," she said affirmingly, "I am a maid from the Rosemen estate. This bucket of fresh water, here, is a gift from Alexander Rosemen to Diana and her family. Please take this and use it however you need." After she finished her script, she just stood there smiling.

"Um.. ok, well..Thank you." Atlas responded.

The maid swiftly left, and a half an hour later Diana returned.

The siblings explained the bucket of water, and Diana tensed up when she understood.

After she cooked dinner and served it, they got a knock at their door.

Diana told them to stay seated, and she went to answer the door. While the two were outside talking, Morgan and Ula were quietly chatting.

"What do you think they're talking about?" Ula asked excitedly.

"I don't know, Ula, it's none of our business." Morgan responded kind of annoyed.

"Well I'm just wondering, you know, I mean, Alexander is really rich..."

"Mind your own business, Ula!" Morgan hissed.

"Why are you so mean?!"

"Because you're so annoying!"

"I'm not annoying, you are!"

"At least I'm not–"

"Shhh!" Atlas hushed.

The door opened and Diana and Alexander stepped in.

"Guys?" Diana asked shyly, "is there any food left for Alexander?"

Her voice was so soft, Atlas barely recognized it.

Why is she?... Then he saw it, the money secretly gripped in Diana's hand. She had it slightly behind her back, but Atlas saw it.

Ula hurriedly grabbed an apple off the window sill and offered it to Alexander.

Diana ignored it, and then offered Alexander half of her meal.

Atlas was disgusted by this, because Diana was horribly skinny and didn't have much on her plate already.

Once the awkward dinner was done, Alexander was ready to leave, but before he did, he shrieked like a little girl because of the creaking house.

Diana opened the door and was ready to wish him a good night, but the door fell off its top hinge.

Alexander squealed again, but this time he had a proposal.

"Diana, how about you and your family move into our guest house? It's about eight times the size of this one and has full time maids."

Atlas saw that Diana was considering the idea, but before she could answer, Ula shouted "yes!"

What?... Atlas thought.

"Come on, Diana!" Ula begged, "this house is falling apart! And his house sounds awesome! Can we, can we?"

Diana hesitated, but then answered "O-Ok."

This can't be happening...

"YYEEESS—" Ula cheered before being cut off by Atlas.

"No!" He shouted in frustration.

"Atlas!" Diana shouted back.

Atlas' glare made eye contact with Alexander.

"Alexander, can you give us some time to think this over?" Atlas asked firmly.

Alexander gave him a scared smile and ran out of the house.

"Seriously, Diana?" Atlas said, "you can't actually be considering this.."

"Really?!" Diana responded, "why not?! If we move in with him, it means a better life!"

"You know he is only offering because you are beautiful! Eventually he is going to propose to you, and what happens after you say no?!"

"Who says I'll say no?"

Atlas' face went dumbfounded, "you can't actually mean that.." He mumbled.

"Yes, I do, because marrying him would give us a ticket out of here! Give us better lives! Don't you want that?"

Atlas just shook his head in response, then said "Well, since you believe you make all of the decisions in this family, do whatever you want."

"Fine! I will!"

Diana started packing up all of her belongings and told Ula to do the same. Before they left, Diana asked Morgan if she wanted to come with, but Morgan said no.

When Diana and Ula were gone, Atlas had a conversation with Morgan.

"Morgan... I have to go..."

"Go where?" Morgan asked worriedly.

"I need to find someone... something..."

"Who?! Or better yet, where?!"

"Morgan..." Atlas sighed.

"No Atlas! You listen to me for once! I have been quiet about everything happening in our family ever since our parents died! We no longer really talk to each other! It doesn't feel like family, more like neighbors that you have to share a room with!

Now, instead of running from every bump in the road... let's just talk."

Atlas slipped on his old jacket, and responded in a low voice, "let's just run one more time." He hurried out of the house, and to the forest.

He ran as fast as he could through the thick overgrowth.

It took him less time to get to the lagoon than it usually does.

When he reached it, no one was there. The lagoon shimmered an empty pale green. Atlas waited by the side and dipped his hand in the water every few minutes. He waited there for a few hours, but Aris never showed.

Atlas cupped a handful of water from the lagoon, and watched it trickle out of his fingers.

He did this over and over again, until he decided to emerge himself. The feeling of the water was so pleasant and serene that it made Atlas forget about all of his troubles. Sitting on the stone ledge and relaxing his head on the moist moss that grew at the edge, he fell asleep.

"Atlas.... Atlas... wake up."

Atlas felt a warm hand on his face, tapping lightly on his left cheek. His eyes fluttered open once he realized who it was.

"A-Aris."

He was staring up at a lovely face with red hair and dazzling brown eyes.

"What are you doing in the Mystic Lagoon all by yourself?" She asked.

"Hm, it was nice." Atlas stated.

Aris gazed down at him lovingly, but then said "you have to go, Atlas, the other mermaids will be here soon and they can't see you."

Aris helped Atlas out of the Lagoon, but before he left, he remembered why he was there.

"Oh! Aris!" Atlas gasped while grabbing her hand, "I remember why I came here! I need your help!"

"With what?" she asked worriedly.

Atlas knelt down next to the Lagoon, keeping intense eye contact with Aris.

"I hate to ask you this... but I need the trident."

Aris ripped her hands out of Atlas' grip and jolted away.

"W-What do you mean?.. The Trident?" Aris asked fearfully.

"I mean the trident! The huge golden fork, that controls the water—"

"SHUSH!" Aris yelled.

Atlas stared at her in silence, while she proceeded to act in a worried manner.

"What?" Atlas asked.

Aris peered around the forest and dipped her head under the water to see if any mermaids were coming. When she declared the coast was clear, she took a deep breath.

"How do you know about the trident?" Aris asked cautiously.

Atlas looked at her like she was mad, but then answered "It was described in a story book that my little–"

"A story book?" Aris asked to clarify.

"Yes, a story book."

"And you want the trident... why?"

Atlas peered into her eyes with a desperate gaze, "I need... It's power..."

Aris' gaze turned into a fearful look, "....I'm sorry..."

Atlas grabbed Aris' shoulder in a fit, "no! Please Aris! You don't understand! I need that trident!"

Before Aris could handle it, a voice popped out in a surprise.

"Take your hands off of her!"

Atlas removed his hands, and looked in the way of the voice. There, on the other side of the lagoon, were two other mermaids.

"Sora, Mia, please, don't get involved..." Aris begged.

"No, Aris!" Sora shouted, "This human has broken many rules! One, he knows the trident exists and wants it. Two, he laid his hands on the Princess of the sea! This is inexcusable behavior at best!"

Atlas looked down at Aris... *Princess?*....

"So what are you going to do?! Arrest him?!"

"Yes! He is under arrest by the Kingdom of the Seven Seas!"

They pushed Aris aside and grabbed Atlas.

Atlas was so stunned, he didn't know what else to do except obey them.

They gave him a magical air bubble that would allow him to breathe freely under water, and dragged him to their kingdom.

They threw him in front of the King, and announced the charges.

The King announced after the charges were read, "This human man will be sentenced to five years in the Underwater prison!"

"But father!" Aris cried out.

"Silence, Aris! This human has crossed his bounds! Guards!"

Four mermen swam up behind Atlas and grabbed his arms.

Atlas struggled "I can't survive underwater!" He yelled.

"We have a special place for humans." One of the guards chuckled.

They led Atlas through a dark passageway, where the water kept getting colder and colder.

Once they passed many dark cells, there was a large one that had no bars.

They threw him in and he quickly landed on a dry, cement floor.

"Uuuggghhh." He groaned in pain as they swam away.

He leaned himself up against the wall and took in a few deep breaths.

He looked around and figured out that he was in a massive air bubble. There were no bars, but if he tried to escape, he would surely drown.

About eight hours later, Triton heard someone whisper his name. He looked at the entrance and saw a beautiful young mermaid with red hair.

"Aris..." Atlas mumbled.

"Hey Atlas... how are you?" She asked shyly.

"Well... not doing great.." He answered pathetically.

"Yeah, I tried talking to my father, but he's incredibly angry."

"What did I even do?!"

Aris hesitated, but then explained. "Many people know about the trident's existence, but saying or even mentioning stealing it, threatens our entire Kingdom. You probably understand why, since you knew if you got it you would have unbelievable power..."

Atlas cupped his face with his hands, "ugh, I still don't understand how that gets me five years in prison!"

"I-I-...It's not really because of that... Saying you want the trident would only get you a meeting with the King so he could scare you..."

Atlas peered up from his hands to look at Aris. "So why am I here?..." He grumbled angrily.

"I-...It's because of me... The one thing that could push my father to sentence you to five years without doing much... Is if he thinks you threatened me in some way."

"Oh..."

There was a moment of silence, until Atlas asked "Why do mermaids and mermen hate humans?"

Aris stared at him for a moment, but then built up the courage to answer.

Aris broke through the air bubble and took a seat on the other side of the cement box, facing Atlas.

She sighed, "It wasn't always like this..." She explained, "Mer-people and humans used to get along, but in the time of my great, great grandmother, humans declared war on our Kingdom. Our relationship with the next generations of humans had been steady, until the time of my mother; Astrid.

When my mother was young; before she met my father, she had a human friend. I believe his name was... Truman. Anyway, he and my mother were great friends. They were even in love with each other, until my mother met my father. When my mother went to tell Truman about my father, Truman was secretly enraged, but still agreed to stay friends with my mother.

A few years passed, and my mother and father were getting married, but my mother made the mistake of telling Truman about it. On their wedding day, Truman and ships of other humans stormed our Kingdom. They destroyed everything, but thankfully most mer-people made it out unharmed.

We rebuilt, and my mother and father still got married. A few months later, she became pregnant with me, her one and only child."

Atlas sat there, dumbfounded.

"How is your mother?" He asked.

Aris hesitated, "...She died a few years ago."

"Oh... I'm so sorry." Atlas apologized.

"No, It's okay, you didn't know."

They sat there across from each other in silence, before Aris got up and swam away.

Atlas felt like an idiot, and just laid in his cell with his hands over his face.

A few months went by, and Aris visited almost every day.

She would sit in his cell with him for hours, just telling each other stories about both worlds. The more Atlas heard about the Sea Kingdom, the more he realized it was better than his world. He also realized with every encounter, how much he loved Aris.

He now noticed things about her that he didn't before. Like the small freckle next to her left eye. Or how she scrunches her nose when she laughs. The way she fidgets with the end of her hair when she talks.

With every conversation, it became more and more about them. More personal.

Atlas began to get comfortable in prison. It may have been dark, cold, and tight, but he didn't feel lonely.

He thought *as long as I can spend every day with her... I'm happy.*

One day, Aris never showed. Atlas didn't think much of it since some days were too risky, but days and days went by, still no Aris.

A whole week went by, and Atlas was worried.

What if something happened to her?

After many days went by, Atlas was greeted by two guards.

"The human man will hereby be granted freedom." They announced.

"Wait...what?!" Atlas shouted in shock.

The guards rolled their eyes, "yes, the King said that you are free. But! You are never to return!"

Atlas always thought he would be happy to hear those words; that he was free. But, never to return? What about Aris? Would he ever see her again?

"Come on." The guards ordered.

They gave him a momentary air bubble, then led him out of the prison. They dropped him off at the shore of his village.

He found his house, and looked inside, but nobody was there.

He searched around, but the house was empty of people and materials. All his sister's clothes were gone, and their other belongings.

For some reason, he expected Morgan to still be there. Then, he acknowledged his foolishness to think that.

He decided to go look for his family at Alexander's estate.

He knocked at Alexander's door, and his maid answered.

"May I help you?" She asked politely.

"Um, yes, are my sisters; Diana, Morgan and Ula here?"

"Oh..." The maid said disheartenedly, "uh, Master Alexander! Diana's brother is at the door!" The maid yelled inside.

A cowardly shriek came from inside, and Atlas rolled his eyes.

A few moments passed, but eventually Alexander came to the door.

"H-hello..." Alexander greeted fearfully.

"Hello," Atlas replied, "I am looking for my sisters. Are they home?"

The blood from Alexander's face drained to his stomach as he looked at Atlas.

"Y-Ya-You mean you don't know...?"

"Know what?" Atlas asked curiously.

Alexander's hands started shaking, "um, uh, I- I- we parted ways."

"Parted ways? What do you mean? You never proposed?"

"Uh... no, I did..."

"Then what happened?"

"It's just... Her face... I mean... It just didn't work out."

Atlas scowled down at him, "where is she?"

"I-I don't know! She left!"

"Tsk..." Atlas scoffed, "Thanks for your help."

Atlas walked out of the estate and made his way to town, to try and find his sisters.

He asked people around the village if they saw his sisters, but none of them had in months.

Atlas was about to make his way back to the house to find clues, but the entire village was interrupted by an obnoxious intrusion.

Horses and soldiers paraded through the town and blew trumpets.

When the musicians ran out of breath, they stopped.

"Herey! Herey! We are here to announce the crowning of our new king! King Adam!"

Everyone cheered, but it was fake. Nobody actually liked King Adam. He has been a pest since he was a child, and everyone remembers. Mouthed off to his father, yelled at people in the streets, and mocked the poor.

"And the first order of the newly crowned king is to knock down the Center Tree and rebuild!"

There was no more cheering, instead a horrified silence.

"No!" An elderly man shouted, "that tree has been here since the beginning of this village! It's a symbol for our people! A symbol of strength! You cannot tear it down!"

Everyone cheered for this man who stood up to the King's soldiers, but their patriotism did not last long.

All of the sudden, an ax sound on wood tore through the town.

Everyone started running to the Center Tree in a panic.

Everybody cried, "why?!"

Once the tree crashed to the ground, the village had a moment of silence for the fallen tree.

Almost immediately, the soldiers chopped the giant tree into pieces and removed it.

After they gathered up the tree, an enormous statue; almost the size of the great tree, replaced it.

They hoisted it up, then bowed down to it.

The villagers were disgusted by the sight of a giant stone statue looking just like the new King Adam.

All the soldiers demanded for the villagers to bow down, but they refused.

"No!" They shouted.

Soldiers then began to throw villagers to the ground, forcing them to bow. It broke out into a huge battle, and Atlas just watched in disgust of his own kind.

Suddenly, all of the soldiers froze to the sound of a carriage's wheels and horses hooves.

Out of the south side of the Center Garden, a black/gold carriage emerged. It stopped near the statue, and a tall handsome man stepped out.

He had longer blonde hair and blue eyes. Dressed in a blue suit with a smug look on his face.

"Hello, men, what is the problem here?" He asked obnoxiously.

"Nothing, Your Majesty, just raising your statue. Isn't it beautiful?" The Commander responded.

"Yes, but I do wish they made it bigger."

Everyone scoffed at his distasteful remark.

"I am so sorry, Your Majesty," The Commander apologizes while kneeling.

"No worries, Commander, as long as I'm the center of everything."

Atlas couldn't take it anymore. This world and its leaders are too conceited and obnoxious. Their stench of rotten secrets lingered with them, making everyone they pass shiver.

Atlas left the scene, not wanting to be involved.

He made his way to the beach, and peered out into the ocean that held the most beautiful Kingdom this world would never have.

The sunlight danced on the ripples of the water, having a party, for they got to travel the current of joy.

Atlas climbed up on a rock and got a better view.

He looked out into the waters, knowing the love of his life was right now swimming in that deep, ocean blue.

It surrounded the lands and stretched for thousands of miles, exceeding the horizon line. It was as great as the skies above, more beautiful than land-dwellers castles and prized possessions, and deeper than the hearts of man.

"That is where I belong..." his lips muttered like the cool breeze, being carried in by the waves.

Atlas ran down to the boat dock and stole one of the fishing boats. A man chased after him, shouting "no! Come back! You can't take that!" But Atlas didn't care.

Atlas sailed deep into the ocean. After searching for hours, he eventually found the Mountain Pillars; mountains that looked like just pillars from above the surface.

Once he passed in between them, he was officially on mer-people territory.

He sailed farther in, without getting caught; because he knew if he did, he would be sent back to prison, and he couldn't let that happen before he saw Aris.

Luckily, a few miles into the Kingdom, he heard an enchanting voice singing not too far from him.

He followed it, and sure enough, the most beautiful voice matched the most beautiful woman.

She was sitting on a rock, combing her hair, singing a lovely song.

"Aris! At last! I have found you!" Atlas cheered.

Aris seemed a bit startled, but once she realized it was Atlas, she was as happy as she could be.

"Atlas! I'm so happy to see you!" She exclaimed as she jumped into the water. She swam to the edge of his boat and he helped lift her up onto the boat.

Aris looked around, "wow, I've never been on a boat before..." She said, amazed.

Atlas looked at the boat, but wasn't nearly as impressed as Aris was. Aris saw it as a beautiful work of art, but all Atlas saw was another thing to keep humans away from the most beautiful place on earth.

"I'm surprised..." Aris admitted, "I'm surprised you came back... Even after everything that's happened..."

"I don't care about any of that. I just wanted to see you."

Aris smiled brightly, "really? I've been wanting to see you too!"

"Really?"

"Yes! Let's spend the day together! We can go back to the Kingdom, I can show you our famous Coral Reef, and I can take you to Dolphin Diner! It's a five starfish restaurant."

"Uh... Aris, I would love to, but you do know I'm banned from the Kingdom... Right?" Atlas responded, confused.

Aris looked at him strangely. "What do you mean? You were never banned..." She stated.

"No, I was. I was told never to come back. I'm sorry if I'm breaking the rules right now, but I needed to see you–"

"You weren't banned! I talked to my father, explained everything, he was a little mad, but he said you were free to go. He never said you were banned!"

"I-I'm sorry Aris, but are you sure the banishment wasn't just implied."

"Yes! My father always says what he is going to do! If you were to be banished, he would have said so!"

Before Atlas could get another word out, Aris jumped over the side of the boat and left.

"Aris!" Atlas shouted overboard.

"Father?" Aris asked firmly when she swam into the Throne Room, where her father sat.

"Yes, my darling?" He replied.

"I have a question."

"And what is your question?"

Aris slightly hesitated, "it's about that man that was here... That human man..."

The King looked at her sternly, "What about him?"

"I have heard that he was banished and I would like to know why."

The King scoffed, "you ask why? You truly do not know the reason?"

Aris glared at him.

"I'll tell you why, Aris, It's because he was a threat to our Kingdom! I had no choice."

"A threat?" Aris scoffed, "No, father, a threat is someone who actually tries to steal the trident."

"You don't know if he was going to try or not, and why is it that you are so obsessed with this human man!"

"Because I love him!" Aris blurted. As soon as she did, her hands covered her mouth.

The King's eyes slowly grew with shock and anger.

"You...what?" The King asked in an unforgiving tone.

"I-I-I love him..."

The King gripped the trident tightly, and Aris felt the water in the room get hotter and hotter.

"Aris!" The King grumbled furiously, "you may not love that human boy! You may only love Edgar!"

"But I don't love Edgar!" She yelled.

"Aris!!" The King yelled back, even more furious than before.

Aris swam out, crying.

She made her way to her Secret Lagoon, so she could be by herself, but forgot that Atlas was still waiting for her.

Atlas was still patiently waiting for Aris to return, but before she did, the boat started to quickly move.

What the... He thought as he watched the water rush by.

He looked at the back of the boat, and saw two mermen pushing the boat.

"Hey!" He shouted at them, "leave my boat alone!"

The mermen did not respond, instead someone else's voice chirped.

"Hello, Atlas."

Atlas looked in the direction of the voice. A merman with a silver tail and black hair was swimming beside the boat, upside down, staring at Atlas.

"Who are you?" Atlas asked.

"Oh me? I'm someone who actually belongs here." The merman answered rudely.

Atlas growled, "where is Aris?!"

"Aris?" The merman repeated, "oh, you shouldn't be concerned with that. She's in good hands."

Atlas gripped the side of the boat angrily, "where. Is. Aris?!" He asked again.

"Again, she's in good hands."

The boat began to slow down and then came to a stop.

"Well," The merman said, "we are out of mer-territory." He then turned to Atlas and glared at him, "If you ever trespass on our territory again, I will have you taken care of."

He was about to swim off, but Atlas chirped "whatever."

"What was that?" The merman asked sternly.

"I said, whatever, because whatever you tell me, I'm still going to find a way to see Aris."

The merman's arms shot out of the water and grabbed ahold of Atlas' shirt, dragging him into the water.

He kept his hold on Atlas' shirt as he growled in his face.

"Look, boy, I don't know who you think you are, but you have no idea who you are messing with."

Without an ounce of fear, Atlas replied "Since I have no idea, how about you tell me."

The merman scowled at him for a few seconds and then announced "I am the Commander of the ocean's greatest army, defender of the Kingdom... And my name is Edgar." He exclaimed proudly, "So, boy, if you think I care about you and your tiny threats, you are sorely mistaken."

Atlas looked into his eyes and chuckled, "well, you cared enough to drag me into the water and tell me your very long title. So.. Edgar, if you think that was going to intimidate me, then YOU are sorely mistaken."

There was a short silence, of just them staring at each other, but all of the sudden, Edgar smiled, however it wasn't a joyful smile, it was a smile that looked as though to say, *I won.*

Edgar started to laugh, then he added, "oh, and I forgot the last part of my title!"

Atlas smiled back arrogantly, "oh really? And what would that be?"

"Not only am I the defender of this Kingdom, but I am also... Princess Aris' fiance."

Edgar burst out laughing at the sight of Atlas' cocky expression turning into sheer confusion.

After a minute of laughing, Edgar's mood abruptly went back to stern. "Now leave, and never come back."

Everything went dark for Atlas, but he ended up waking up on a beach.

It wasn't the same beach he usually came to, he actually has never seen this beach.

Instead of a forest beyond the sand, it was a cliff. It was a cliff for as far as he could see, almost like a wall guarding this beach; or whatever lay on the other side.

He decided to walk along the beach until he saw a village or something he recognized.

He walked for hours, until he finally came by some woods.

He thought he might find a village through those woods, so he started to travel through them.

About thirty minutes had passed, but still no luck.

He was so tired that he sat on a log and fell asleep.

An unknown amount of time went by, but a deep, raspy voice told him, "I wouldn't sleep there if I were you."

Atlas' eyes twitched open, to where he could make out a blurry figure in front of him.

"Wh– who are you?" Atlas asked.

The figure didn't answer.

Atlas shook his head and his vision came back.

He saw a tall, slender looking man, wearing a black suit and a black hat, standing in front of him.

Atlas flinched, but then noticed the man wasn't that scary, except for his eyes, his eyes glowed yellow.

The mysterious man was about to walk away, but Atlas stopped him. "Wait! Who are you?"

The mysterious man sighed, but then replied "I am no friend, nor foe."

Then he really walked away. Atlas chased him, but couldn't keep up with him. It was as if this man could skim through existence, because he was gone in a flash.

Atlas looked around, but couldn't see where he went.

He then just followed a random direction, until he stumbled across a little cottage that was built in between two trees.

There was smoke coming out of the chimney, so someone must have been inside.

Maybe that's where that man lives.... Atlas thought. He went up to the door and was about to knock, when the same voice said from behind him, "don't knock."

Atlas turned around to find the same mysterious man.

"Why not?" Atlas asked.

The man sighed in slight irritation, "because if you knock, it will be answered."

Atlas tilted his head curiously, "and what's wrong with that?"

There was a quick moment of silence, where only the sound of the wind rustling the leaves could be heard.

"Because you do not want what he has to offer." The man answered.

Atlas didn't understand why, but he believed him.

"Okay." Atlas responded, "Then what do I want?"

The man took a step closer to Atlas and handed him a piece of rolled up paper. Once he did, the man disappeared, along with the cottage.

Atlas felt a shiver run up his spine. He slowly, then quickly, backed away from where the cottage used to be.

He ran further into the woods, with no idea where he was headed.

Once he ran out of energy, he knelt beside a large willow tree.

He unrolled the paper that was given to him and it read:

4121 Logwood Trail, Forest
Bring something to trade.

Atlas was confused about what this meant.

Forest? Is that even a town?

Atlas headed in a random direction, and hoped for the best.

Days went by, until he stumbled upon a peaceful river that flowed pleasantly through the forest. He instantly felt thirsty, so he knelt down to get a drink. He cupped his hands full of water and drank from his hands. All of the sudden, he hears the rushing of water coming closer and closer. He was so captivated by how calm the water was, he didn't expect such a flood to occur. Before he could get out of the way, a surge of water came crashing over him.

He was swept away by the current and dragged for what seemed like miles.

He woke up, aching from head to toe, at the side of the now flowing river.

He struggled to climb to his feet, but when he did, he saw he was deeper in the forest than he once was. There were so many trees that the sun barely shone through.

He looked around to find a path, but the only thing that caught his eye was a tiny log cabin. It looked poorly built, but there were windows and smoke rising out of the roof.

Atlas made his way over there, but when he came closer, he noticed a sign posted near the entry that said , '4121 Logwood Trail, Forest'.

"Huh!" Atlas gasped, remembering that address from the note.

He eagerly ran up to the door and knocked.

A few minutes passed, but a small, bearded man answered.

He wore a green shirt and a long, droopy, red hat.

He didn't look too happy, but he quickly asked "what is it that you need?"

Atlas was slightly taken off guard by how instinctively he asked that, but he was glad he asked.

"Well... I want to be... A merman." Atlas hesitantly stated, knowing it sounded ridiculous, but the little man didn't seem phased at all.

"Well," he said in his high pitched, grumbling voice, "I can do that, but I need something in return."

Right then, Atlas remembered the second part of the note, 'bring something to trade'.

Atlas frantically searched for something for him to trade, but the little man exclaimed "no, no, not an object..."

Atlas was confused, not sure what he meant by that.

The little man stated "You are never to return to land again. You may not even get close enough to touch the sand."

"What?!" Atlas shouted.

"Yes, you can never return."

"B-B-But I don't understand, you wouldn't profit from that at all!"

"Don't you tell me what I do and do not profit from! I make the rules for the trade and you follow them! That's the deal."

Atlas took a few minutes to think about this, but the little man tempted "would you rather have your sweet land and legs.... Or the love of your life? It's your choice."

Atlas thought what got him into this situation at first. The reason he searched for Aris at the beginning was because he needed strength and power to provide a wonderful home and life for his family. Now, he didn't care about power.

Atlas took a few more moments to decide, but eventually answered "Aris... I need Aris."

"Excellent!" The little man exclaimed excitedly. The little man closed the door, leaving Atlas by himself. About two minutes went by when Atlas felt something watching him. He looked at a window at the side of the house, and just saw a flash of blonde. *Someone is there...* Atlas thought. Right before Atlas was about to look through the window, his attention was pulled by the little man opening the door. "Alright," the little man said, "the deal is sealed."

The little man snapped his fingers and Atlas collapsed on the ground when half his body became fish. He was told by the little man that he should go into the river.

Atlas slithered his way over to the river, and was carried away by its current.

Atlas dunked his head underwater, but he could still breathe! It was amazing!

The oxygen underwater felt thicker, but it was still easy to breathe.

It took awhile, but he finally made it to the ocean. He had been sort of practicing swimming with his tail in the river, but he still struggled when he met the ocean.

Once he got the feel for it, he made his way to mer-territory.

It took him several hours, but thankfully he made it.

Mermaids and mermen swam around happily, not realizing that he was a foreigner.

His goal was to make it to the castle and find Aris, but he got distracted by so many things.

Mermen riding seahorses, shops selling jellyfish—jelly and what they called 'sunlight in a bottle'. What was really intriguing was the pet shop, selling stingrays and blowfish.

Even though difficult, Atlas gained focus on the goal.

He swam a few miles, then reached the palace.

He only saw guards at the gates and also stationed at the other entry points.

He cautiously made his way around the gates, but soon realized that was a mistake.

During his quick scan of the castle, he failed to notice the guards hiding behind the coral reef a few yards away from the gate.

The guards yelled "hey, you!" and began chasing Atlas, who was swimming towards the castle.

Atlas swam to the smallest entrance, guarded by only one guard.

He knocked the guard aside and made it into the castle.

The other two guards were still chasing him, but luckily for Atlas, there were many corners to duck behind.

One hallway led Atlas to a hole in the ceiling, which led to the upstairs.

Ah, of course... Atlas thought, *merfolk don't use stairs!...*

He followed the many ceiling holes until he reached a floor that looked a lot different from the rest.

This floor was covered in glowing coral covering the walls.

He had a good feeling about this one, so he swam down it.

He passed a few darkly colored doors, until he heard voices a little further down the hall.

Once he reached them, he found that they were coming from a slightly opened door.

He widened the crack a bit more and looked through. There were two mermen talking to each other aggressively, but surprisingly, one sounded familiar.

The familiar voice was coming from the merman who had his back facing door, so Atlas couldn't make out who it was.

"I can't believe you failed! A sunfish could've accomplished it!"

Atlas heard through the door.

"Sorry sir, but his guard came in. If I put the poison in the cup–"

"Silence you fool! Someone could hear us!"

"Sorry, sir..."

Poison?... Atlas thought. His heart was pounding, *I shouldn't be here...*

Atlas was about to keep swimming when he heard, "I need to get rid of the King before Aris finds somebody else..."

Aris? What does he want with Aris?...

"Sir... the Princess will never find anybody but you, the King loves you."

"I know he does, that fool, but I know Aris doesn't. She has her eyes on this human boy. I already threw him out, but it's only a matter of time before she finds him again. If she's not forced to marry me now, then I'll never be King!"

How dare he?! Atlas was about to knock open the door and punch that merman in the face! But he couldn't... He knew he would never see Aris again if he did that.

Instead, Atlas needed to make sure this guy's plan didn't work.

Atlas made his way to a giant throne room, hiding in the shadows away from the guards. He snuck around for a bit, until the King and Aris entered the throne room.

"But father, I don't want to marry him!" Aris exclaimed.

"Don't be ridiculous darling, he is a good merman. He is the head of my noble guards and so was his father! He comes from a strong family bloodline, and if you bear a son, he can become a noble guard! You'd make your family proud."

"But... I don't love him..." Aris replied, bitterly.

Her father faced her and responded, "You'll learn to love him. So don't worry so much about it. Now, if you will, please get ready for the banquet tonight, I'll speak to you again later."

Her father swam away, leaving Aris in the middle of the throne room, alone.

"Aris!" Atlas loudly whispered.

Aris looked around.

"Aris!" Atlas whispered again.

She finally looked in his direction and gasped.

"Atlas!" She exclaimed happily, with a lot of confusion.

He swam over to her and they hugged.

"You have a tail!" She shrieked.

"I had to... I needed to see you again..." He responded.

"B-but how...?"

"That doesn't matter, look, I have something I need to tell you."

"Princess!" A woman's voice cried out.

"Oh no! That's my seamstress, you need to hide." Aris said as she hurried Atlas into a hiding place.

"B-but, Aris, I have something I need to tell you–"

"Later! You can't get caught!"

She shoved Atlas into a dark corner, but before she rushed away, she sweetly kissed his cheek.

"I'll see you later." She giggled as she hurried away to the calling of her name.

Atlas watched in awe of her, until she disappeared into an upstairs hallway.

Atlas wandered in the shadows of the castle, not knowing what else to do. His heart ached to be with Aris, but he knew it wasn't possible. *Or was it?...*

He thought back to Aris and her father's conversation, *they mentioned a banquet tonight!*

If it's a banquet, that means there will be a lot of people.

Perfect. Nobody will notice me.

He continued to swim down a random hallway, but eventually heard the same two voices from behind the door.

They seemed to be coming down the same hallway, so Atlas had to find somewhere to blend in. There were no rooms to go into, so he had to find something else.

The voices were getting closer and closer, so he decided to test his luck and hide on the ceiling. The hallway had high ceilings and was dimly lit, so he had a chance.

He pressed his back against the rough material, and was looking down.

While the voices passed him, he heard "During the banquet. Make sure to put it in the right cup, I will not forgive another screw up."

They're gonna kill the King at the banquet! I need to stop that from happening!

Once they were far enough away, Atlas continued down the hallway.

He finally found an empty, unlocked room.

It had a golden interior, but it didn't seem to have anything inside it, only two closet doors.

Atlas opened them to see what was inside and found merman clothes.

The one that stuck out to him was a black suit with a bow tie.

Perfect... He thought as he tried it on.

That night a bunch of mermaids and mermen swarmed into the banquet room and mingled.

While everyone was distracted by the different conversations around them, Atlas made his way into the crowd.

He was wearing a white shirt, black suit jacket and black bow tie, for mermen. He had also found a strange substance that felt like hair gel, so he rubbed his wavy dark, brown hair with it, pushing it out of his face.

While making his way through the crowd, he got several flirty glances from the mermaids, but he didn't care, the only mermaid he wanted was Aris.

After an hour of mingling, a voice announced through the room, "please take your seats, dinner will be served."

Everyone hurried to their assigned seats, then Atlas realized he didn't have a seat!

He looked around and thankfully found an empty seat by a sad looking mermaid.

I have to make this work... He said to himself.

He swam over to the sad mermaid and said "hello, why are you so grim?" He asked while slyly sitting in the seat next to her.

"Oh," she said, "I was supposed to meet a merman here, but he didn't show up..."

She looked down at her lap in disappointment. She had orange hair and a purple tail. She was wearing a matching skirt and was dressed up in chunky jewelry.

"Well," Atlas replied "that man obviously doesn't know what he's missing out on."

The mermaid looked up in surprise, then blushed shyly.

This is perfect. I get this seat and can also cheer this poor mermaid up. He thought to himself.

He continued to lightly flirt with the mermaid and eventually got her name, it was Sophia.

For dinner, they had grilled salmon and salad. The whole time Atlas kept trying to figure out how they grilled in the bottom of the ocean, but he eventually let it go when he saw Aris.

Her red hair looked extra flowy, and she was wearing a green and white skirt with her green tail. On top of her head she presented a golden crown with a single ruby in the center.

Beautiful... Atlas thought as he gazed at her.

Another voice announced, "welcome, King Jonas!"

Everyone stood and clapped their hands when the King came out to sit on his throne. Once he sat down, so did everyone else.

Aris was beside him and whispered something in his ear. The King made a swooshing gesture with his hand and she rolled her eyes.

The same voice announced "now, please, enjoy yourselves with a dance."

There was a large space in front of the King for dancing, and a band was playing at the side of the room.

Sophia popped up and exclaimed "come dance with me!"

She grabbed his hand and pulled him out of his chair.

They went to the dance floor with many other couples and danced to the music in front of the King and the Princess.

Sophia was having a great time, but Atlas was uncomfortable.

He and Aris made eye contact, but she looked away.

While they were all dancing, a waiter came out with a singular drink to hand to the King.

When Atlas saw the cup, he immediately remembered that those two men had planned to poison it.

Atlas gasped as the cup was handed to the King and rushed to knock it out of his hand.

"No!" He shouted as he slapped it. The wine spilled into the water and floated around.

"What are you doing?!" The King yelled.

Everyone gasped at Atlas' actions, but Atlas shouted "nobody touch that wine! It's poisoned!"

Everybody gasped again.

As the King rose to bring judgment upon Atlas, Edgar came out.

"Let me take him, my King. I'll handle it."

As he reached to grab Atlas' arm, Aris argued "no! Don't do it!"

She swatted the commander's hand and stood in between them, guarding Atlas.

"Aris, what are you doing?" The King asked.

"Yes, Aris, what are you doing?" Edgar parroted.

"I'm protecting the actual noble one." She snapped back.

"What do you mean? this man is a criminal." Edgar exclaimed.

"No he's not, you are, Edgar."

Edgar gasped, "how dare you? I am the commander of this Kingdom's army, your father's most trusted guard, and most importantly your fiance!"

Aris rolled her eyes, "those are just titles, I know who you really are."

"Aris, enough." The King ordered, "you will respect Edgar's authority and hand over this fool."

"Don't you understand, father? You're being brainwashed! You think he's so trustworthy and noble, but he tried to poison you!"

Edgar dramatically held his hand over his heart as though someone just broke it.

"Aris! I will not toler–"

An archer took his position and aimed at the King. The arrow shot down from the balcony and quickly made its way through the water. The King and Princess were distracted, but both Atlas and Edgar saw it. Atlas pushed Aris out of the way and slid in front of the King, taking the arrow to the side.

Unlike Atlas, Edgar backed up when he saw the arrow headed toward the King, and thankfully everyone noticed.

Blood gushed into the water from Atlas' side, and Aris hurried doctors over to help.

While the King was being moved to safety, he said two things.

"He saved me." and, "Guards! Arrest Edgar!"

Atlas woke up in a brightly lit room. He had bandages on his left side and was lying on a bed.

He heard Aris' voice right outside of his room. She was asking the doctor if she could see him. The doctor answered, "of course, Princess Aris."

She came into the room and gazed down at him. Her hand folded in on his and he grabbed it.

"I have good news." She said sweetly.

"Oh yeah? What's that?" He responded.

"My father said you can stay in out world, if you'd like. I know you might not want to after this, but..."

"I'd love to stay here."

"Really?" She asked, shocked.

He nodded, "this place is much better than in the human world."

She chuckled, "Oh, I'd hate to know what happened to you there."

They both laughed, but Atlas had to stop because it hurt his side.

"Aris..."

"Yes?"

"I know this isn't really the place to ask you this... But, will you marry me?"

She squeezed his hand and answered "there is no other man I'd say yes to."

"What about Edgar?"

"Shut up."

They both laughed again.

With the King's blessing, a few months later was Atlas and Aris' wedding.

Aris dressed in a beautiful white gown and veil, and Atlas wore the same suit he wore at the banquet.

Since there was an arrow hole in the side, the maid pleaded that he wear a different one, but for his own reasons, he said no.

As Aris made her way down the aisle, Atlas watched in amazement wondering, *how could any woman or mermaid be that beautiful?*

They both said their "I do's", and became husband and wife.

Later that year, Atlas was crowned the King of the Seven Seas. First, he settled the relationship between the land kingdom and them, allowing the land kingdom to fish freely. Secondly, he imprisoned Edgar in the Mariana Trench's prison cell for treason, along with his accomplices. Lastly, and most personal, he took immediate action by banishing his sister, Diana, from the Kingdom's territory, after she tried to steal the trident from his hands at coronation.

I guess that's twice he chose Aris over his own flesh and blood...

Chapter Six

B rown and green were the only colors that were shown in this rejected land. There might have been gray in the rocks, except mud from boots of the goblins covered them.

This land of the goblins was overpopulated, but nobody could tell from the surface; not that anybody ever visited.

Goblins had made tunnels through the ground, that was their only way to escape the beasts that lurked just outside their poorly built wall.

"What are goblins good for?!" protestors argued during the Get Goblins Out era.

"All they do is smell bad and take up food! They are too lazy and too dumb to do anything useful!"

After about a half a decade, the protestors of the Get Goblins Out movement won. All goblins of every kingdom were banished. This was because there was a huge famine going on and several goblins were found stealing food.

Now, goblins live in an abandoned part of the forest. Ever since they moved there, for the last couple of centuries, no outsider has ever stopped by.

A little goblin was on the surface and staring at the wall.

"Rumpel, what are you doing?!" His mother called out to him in worry.

"Sorry, mama, I just wanted to see it..." He answered.

"You know the rules," she scolded, "no goblin is to get within thirty feet of the wall! There are beasts that want to harm us!"

"But mama... I wasn't doing anything..."

"Hey kid!" An officer goblin shouted, "Get away from that wall!"

His mama picked him up and carried him back to the "village".

"You know the rules, kid." The officer rebuked.

"Sorry..."

"I'll handle him, officer." his mama promised. Mama took the little goblin back to their underground tunnel.

"But mama, I want to see beyond–"

"No, Rumple!" His mama snapped back.

After fifteen minutes of squeezing through a crowd of goblins, they finally made it to their home. The goblins called these tunnels that held homes, tunnelments. There were rows of wooden doors lining the dirty tunnel. On each door were numbers, sort of like addresses.

They opened their wooden door into their tunnelment. The whole thing was one room. Crammed into it was an oven that barely ever got used, because there was no place for the smoke to go. Not like there were windows underground. In the corner were two beds, one smaller than the other, and stuffed into another corner was an old, red couch; which papa was sitting on, reading the newspaper.

"Hello, honey." Mama said to papa.

"Hello, darling." Papa said back.

"What's in the paper today?" Mama asked.

"Well," Papa adjusted his glasses, "apparently, the Cement family just had another little one."

"Oh, Russel, I've already heard about that all day! It's all anybody can talk about!"

"Ok, ok, sorry. Oh! How about this? Brick's son was apparently sent to the hospital this morning!"

"Why? What happened?"

"He had an ear infection."

"Oh, that poor thing, I hope he's ok." Mama exclaimed as she washed some dishes.

"Is there anything else, papa?" Rumple asked.

"Ummm," Papa hummed as he scanned the paper, "weather will be rainy.... King Stone and his Queen Gem are adopting a new dog..."

"Oooh, gossip." mama chimed in.

"What do you mean by gossip?" Rumple asked.

Mama set the plate and dish towel down and muttered "well, you didn't hear this from me, but my co-worker, Poppy, said that her friend Cargo, has a niece named Ruby, who is dating a male named Frier, who may know the dog trainer that the Royals are buying from. Who may have a secret spouse, who may be related to the Green family." Then mama went back to the dishes with a smirk on her face.

"Ooohhh, that is a good scoop." Papa replied.

Rumple groaned in boredom, as he laid on his bed.

"What's with you?" Mama asked.

"I'm so bored! There's nothing to do here!"

"That's not true!" Mama replied.

"Yes it is! The most exciting news we've gotten this week is that some goblin may have a secret spouse!"

"So what?" Mama exclaimed, "Do you need frogs flying around for you to be entertained?!"

Rumple sat up in his bed, "no! I'm just saying that every day here seems to be the same! Every day we read in the paper that some goblin got sick, or some goblin got married, or King Stone and his Queen are doing something."

"Actually," Papa chirped in, "no goblins have gotten married today. Rose and Tiles' wedding is tomorrow."

"Oh, speaking of that, we need to get a gift for them."

And just like that, mama and papa got distracted by daily life.

Rumple laid in his bed, staring up at the ceiling as his parents discussed what to get the new couple.

What's beyond that wall?... He wondered. He could only imagine the smell of fresh air. It must not always have a hint of smoke, or the lingering stench of goblin armpit.

To be free and able to stretch out your arms without hitting any goblin. He only had that feeling for a few minutes by the wall, before his mama grabbed him.

He wondered what it would be like to escape the beasts on the other side of the wall, and run off to a far away Kingdom. One like they learned about in school.

A few more days passed by, with boring news as usual. When Rumple got back from school, his papa was excited to read him that day's news.

"Rumple! You won't believe it! The King and Queen are expecting a special guest!"

"A special guest?" Rumple repeated, intrigued.

"Yes! This is history! This land hasn't had any guests since... since... forever!"

"That's great, papa! Who is it?"

"Um.. I'm not sure.. It doesn't say."

"Oh wow! This must be some surprise!" Rumple cheered. Finally, something interesting.

"When is the guest going to be here?" Rumple asked.

"It says he's coming tomorrow!"

"Oh boy! I'm so excited! I wonder who it could be!"

That night Rumple was so excited that he couldn't sleep. At the crack of dawn he was out of his bed, changing into his nicest clothes. He made sure not to wake his parents, by being quieter than his papa's snoring.

He snuck out of his tunnelment, and made his way outside.

He was expecting a large crowd that did the same as he did, but he was the only one.

He knew that goblins were known for sleeping, since there was nothing in their lives to get up for, except for school and jobs, but today was special!

Rumple looked around, and out of nowhere he heard a loud *CHIRP!*

He flinched at the unknown sound.

What is that?... he wondered as he looked around.

He heard it again, *CHIRP!* He flinched.

He looked up at the sky and saw a bird.

CHIRP! The bird called out.

What in the world?... Birds make sounds?!... He thought in amazement. He's never heard a bird chirp before. The town has always been so loud with goblins, that he's never known any animal—except for dogs making sounds!

Rumple started walking around the town, enjoying the peace and quiet.

He went down alleyways and the streets, not seeing a single goblin during his walk. He took a deep breath in and out, feeling a kind of peace that he's never felt before.

"Hey, you there." An unknown voice said.

Rumple jumped in panic. "Who? Me?" asked in fear. He started to look around, but couldn't spot where it was coming from.

"Right here." The voice directed.

Rumple looked towards one of the buildings, and saw a mysterious creature. One that he's only seen in a book.

Is that a...a... human?... Rumple thought in astonishment.

The human started walking closer to him, but Rumple backed up in fear.

"There is no reason to be afraid of me, boy." The human said.

For some reason, Rumple believed him after that.

"Who are you?" Rumple asked.

"Well, I'm the special guest."

Rumple just gawked at him.

"I have to say, I was expecting a bigger welcome, but this will do."

The human had on a brown robe, and had a long white beard.

Rumple stared at him in amazement, as the human looked around. "Is there somewhere I can park my cart?" The human asked, bringing out a small wooden cart, filled with random things.

"Um, of course!" Rumple exclaimed, "you can put it anywhere."

"Wonderful." The human responded.

The human dragged his cart over to a boulder and sat down.

"This is the perfect spot to sell my things!"

"What are you selling?" Rumple asked curiously.

"Well... why don't you have a look?" The human replied.

Rumple carefully uncovered a vase and looked inside.

"Ah!" He shouted and tumbled backwards. "What are those?!" He asked in fear.

The human chuckled loudly, "those are witches eyeballs!" He exclaimed, "very rare, and very expensive."

"Who would want to buy those?" Rumple asked as he dusted himself off.

The human thought for a moment, "wizards, other witches, and collectors."

"Hm." Rumple replied as he looked inside a silver bowl.

"What's this?" Rumple asked.

It was a green jelly, with what seemed like pebbles emerged inside.

"Oh, now that is a find. It's called Giant's jelly. Scooped from the pit of a giant's stomach."

"Ew, no wonder it smells bad." Rumple said, putting the lid back on. "Do you have anything that didn't get taken from a living creature?" Rumple asked.

"Hm, well..." The human mumbled as he searched through his cart.

"Ah, these." The human said, taking out a tiny, brown bag.

"I found these at a pawn shop in Oaksland."

"What's a pawn shop?" Rumple asked.

The human squinted at Rumple, curious of his ignorance. "Well, a pawn shop is a store where you can trade things for other things." The human explained.

"Interesting." Rumple mumbled, "hold on a second!" Rumple yelled as he ran away.

He ran back to his tunnelment and quietly searched through his belongings. Once he found what he was looking for, he ran back to the human.

"Do you trade?" Rumple asked, out of breath.

"Of course I trade!" The human responded.

Rumple stuck out his hand and opened his closed fist carefully, as though what he was holding was magic.

When the human looked down, he saw that it was nothing but a red feather.

"It is my most prized possession." Rumple admitted, "I found it near the wall, but I had never seen anything like it."

The human looked down at the feather again, and took pity on the poor goblin.

You see, the human has spent his whole life traveling the world and has seen everything there is to see, however this little goblin is so encased in this one, overcrowded territory, that he treats a simple red feather as though it was treasure.

The human looked down at Rumple and asked "what do you want most in this world?"

Rumple looked confused, but then answered "I want to see what is outside these walls."

The human nodded, "then," He said as he grabbed something out of his cart, "I will trade you that feather for this."

He held up a pointy, maroon colored hat.

"This is a hat made of a fairies dress and stitched together with the hair of a wizard's beard." The human presented, gazing at the item, as it was one of a kind. "Masterfully crafted on Mount Ouranos, then laid out on two bars of gold under the Northern Lights, to absorb the magic of the universe. Truly, one of a kind."

Rumple gazed up at the hat in amazement, "wow... That's worth this feather?...." Rumple asked, with an astonished yet puzzled expression.

"Well, is that feather important to you?" The human asked in reply.

"Yes." Rumple answered without hesitation, "I've had it for years... It's the only thing that's ever kept me from suffocating in this crowded place."

The human smirked and gestured to the hat, "well, now you get to leave..."

Rumple glanced back and forth from his feather to the hat.

Hmmm, He wondered, *should I? This could be my only chance... but it could be a mistake...*

Hesitantly, he handed his red feather over to the human's hand.

With an affirmative nod, the human took the feather and gave Rumple the maroon hat.

He grabbed it with two hands and held it close to him, just like he did the feather. What was once his greatest treasure, now, no longer even in thought.

The minute he put the hat on his head, he felt a burst of energy and confidence. A feeling of power surged through him, as he headed towards the wall that once blocked him from the outside world.

He jumped to get far up on the wall, but the power inside of him boosted his jump. He landed on the top of the wall, and gave a quick look behind him to his old village. Then, he looked in front of him and saw the open world. A forest that seemed like it would never end, laid out in front of him.

With one final leap, Rumple made his way into the unknown.

As Rumple wandered through the forest, flinching at every strange sound and collecting everything that he'd never seen before, he found a river.

Rumple went to the edge of the rushing river to get a drink.

When he cupped the water in his hands and lowered his head a bit to sip it, a salmon jumped up and hit his head, making his hat slip off into the water.

"No!" Rumple shouted as his hat was washed away.

He jumped in after it and the water carried him away.

He fought to get his head above water, but that didn't keep the water from rushing into his nose and mouth.

After about five minutes of being pushed down stream, his shirt got caught on a fallen tree.

The exhaustion of struggling in the river, and being repeatedly hit by rocks, knocked Rumple unconscious. Luckily, his head was above water so he could still breathe.

About thirty minutes passed by, before a group of knights came across Rumple caught on the tree.

They hoisted him up and tied him to the back of one of their white horses.

After two hours of traveling, they finally made it to a kingdom.

Rows of cottage looking homes lined the streets. In a pattern like a spider's web, the streets were formed around the Kingdom, with a palace in the center. The palace was white, gray and light pink, with shimmering crystals lapping around the five towers.

Rumple was jolted awake when the knights jumped off their horses and were taking off the carts, which were full of jewels.

Once he woke up, one of the knights gestured for Rumple to follow him.

Confused, Rumple followed the knight, who didn't talk much.

"Um, excuse me?" Rumple politely asked.

"Yes?" The knight responded.

Rumple looked around as they walked through the stable.

The horses peaking their heads out of their stalls terrified Rumple.

"AH!" He shouted, as a horse stretched his head out to sniff him.

"What's the matter?!" The knight asked, almost drawing his sword as he turned around.

"What are those!" Rumple asked frantically, pointing at the horse.

"Horses?" The knight exclaimed.

"H-h-horses....?" Rumple muttered, "I've never heard of them be-fore...."

"Seriously?" The knight questioned, shocked.

They made their way out of the stable, and walked up the pathway to the palace.

Almost twenty guards were posted in front of the giant gate.

They halted Rumple, but the knight murmured something to the guards and they were allowed to pass.

A large chain was cranked in order to open up the massive gate. Behind it, was a long red carpet, leading to stairs, which led to two large, glass doors.

Once they made it to the glass doors, they were opened for them by two fancy dressed men.

The whole palace was painted in light colors, the same colors that were shown outside. Many large, detailed windows hung in the en-trance, and brightened up the already bright walls.

"Follow me." The knight ordered.

They walked through two white doors, with beautiful floral design carved into them.

Behind the doors, were marble stairs leading down to a marble ball room. Marble floors, with marble pillars, holding up balconies on both sides. The ceiling was painted intricately, with baby cupids resting on clouds, on a golden background. In the center, an enormous, golden chandelier hung down, creating a sparkling, warm glow.

Rumple looked around in amazement, because he's never seen any-thing like it.

While his attention was focused on the beauty of the marble and elaborate paintings, he didn't notice somebody on the left balcony, overlooking them.

"Who are you?" A woman, standing on the balcony asked.

When the knight noticed that the woman was the Queen, he immediately bowed.

"Your Majesty, forgive me, but I didn't know where to bring this foreigner. We found him in the river, unconscious and close to drowning."

The Queen was a tall, slim woman, who wore a black dress that stuck out among the bright colors.

The Queen stared at Rumple for a minute, before she said "come up here, I have an idea."

The knight hopped up and led Rumple to the staircase.

They met the Queen in a large room, with old looking artwork covering the walls.

The knight pushed down on Rumple's right shoulder, making him bow in front of the Queen.

"So, you were found in a river, hm?" The Queen inquired.

Rumple answered "Uh, yes, ma'am."

"Your majesty!" The knight harshly whispered.

"I mean, Your Majesty!" Rumple squealed.

The Queen gave a slight chuckle, then asked "what is your name, boy?"

Rumple lowered his head and replied "My name is quite odd, so everybody calls me Rumple."

The Queen seemed satisfied with that answer, then ordered him to stand.

When Rumple and the knight got off their knees, the Queen exclaimed "welcome to our Kingdom, Rumple!" As she stretched out her arms, like a performer does before the show begins.

The Queen looked at the knight and said "you can leave now. I'll take care of Rumple."

The knight followed orders and left the room at once.

The Queen waved her hand, as to motion Rumple to follow her.

He followed closely behind as they walked further into the palace.

They went up a spiraling staircase that was tucked away behind a closed door, as though it wasn't supposed to be seen.

At the top of the stairs, was the most spacious and dark room that Rumple had seen in that palace.

There were large, window shaped holes in the walls circling the oval shaped room.

The floor was a black tile, and the walls were made out of black and purple stone. Along with the natural light, there were also lit torches hanging on the walls.

The only furniture residing in the room was a gray colored table that held random items. Such as a brush, a crystal box and a little glass bottle that was filled with a clear liquid. However, the one thing in the room that kept catching Rumple's attention was a sizable, purple cloth hanging on the wall, obviously hiding something.

"What is this place?" Rumple asked curiously.

"Oh, this is just someplace I like to come to." The Queen replied, "I love the view."

Rumple looked out of the opening in the wall and saw the whole town. It looked so small from far away, and Rumple had never seen anything like it.

"Wow..." He uttered.

The Queen pointed out of the opening and stated "If you look over the town, you can see the forest. And about a hundred miles from here into the forest, is where you are from, correct?"

Her gaze turned from outside to Rumple, who was standing there with a puzzled expression.

"You know where I'm from?" He inquired.

"Oh come on," The Queen exclaimed, "you don't exactly blend in. Anybody could tell that you are a goblin."

Rumple lowered his head, like he was ashamed.

"I'm surprised that you made your way out of the territory," The Queen continued, "isn't that against the law?"

Rumple started shaking, as she made him out to be a criminal.

"It's not illegal, it's just frowned upon." He explained.

She scoffed, "It may only be frowned upon by the goblins, however it's illegal for a Kingdom to house any of your kind since the Get Goblins Out movement. You've been banished from every land except your own."

"I-I-I..." Rumple tried to speak through his fear, "I didn't mean to cause any trouble... It's just..."

"Oh no, darling!" The Queen interrupted, "you didn't cause any trouble! It was your ancestors that caused the trouble."

Her high pitched voice that started out that sentence, came to a lower tone at the end.

"Why do you seem mad?" Rumple asked with an innocent tone of voice.

"Because the depression was all you stupid, goblins fault!" She shouted in hate.

Rumple flinched backwards, and fell on his bottom.

She took slow steps toward him, but he tried to crawl away. He scrambled for the steps to get away, and when he reached them, she yelled "guards! Get him!"

He ran down the stairs as fast as he could, and from many different directions, he heard the pounding of the feet getting closer. He sprinted down one of the hallways and went through the first unlocked door he could find.

He was in a small, storage room that had a little window ahead of him.

The guards came to stand still at the other side of the door, as though they could smell that he was inside.

He swiftly locked the door, and the moment he did they started trying to knock it down. It was only a matter of minutes before they busted the door down, so he only had one option.

With a shiny rock that he found in the storage room, he threw it at the window and it shattered.

Luckily, due to his body size, he was able to squeeze through the little opening.

When he looked down, his guts knotted together.

It was many stories up, with the ground beneath him being completely stone.

Before he was able to squeeze back into the room, the guards had knocked down the door.

"Get him!" They shouted.

Rumple ducked behind the wall, holding onto a gemstone with his fingertips and having both of his feet pressing tightly onto divots in the wall.

He had never been rock climbing, but he had heard stories when he was younger from his great grandpa. Great grandpa had made it sound more exciting and less terrifying than it actually was, but even though he was hanging on for dear life, he found time to laugh at how adventurous this was.

The guards couldn't fit through the small window, so Rumple was able to take his time. Carefully searching for holes in the wall, or gemstones to grab onto.

He slowly made his way to the next window, but when he peeked inside, he found two guards waiting for him.

"Oops!" Rumple shouted as he jolted back, when the guard reached his hand out to grab him.

Rumple lost his footing, but still hung from gripping the stone above him.

He desperately hung on, until he found his feet placements.

He couldn't go through the window, nor could he go past the window.

The guard was still trying to reach him, but his arm wasn't long enough.

Rumple looked up to see if there was anything he could grab a hold of, but the only thing there was was too high.

"Maybe if I jumped for it..." He murmured to himself.

He glanced back at the guard waiting for him, then glanced back up to the gemstone above him.

Then he whispered to himself a countdown, "three...two.....one!" and he sprung himself as high as he could, and almost grabbed it, but he slipped.

"Ahhhhh!" He screamed as he fell.

He fell two stories down, but fortunately, he fell onto a small window sill that stuck out.

He was about to roll off of it, but he snatched a hold of it, and pulled himself up.

He pressed his back as hard as he could against the glass, and looked down. He felt exhilarated, but also exhausted and out of breath, however his breathing didn't slow down, as he sucked in air, quickly releasing it. His legs felt numb, but they quaked, and his hands felt dry but they were sweating. It was such a strange feeling that he had never felt before, but he loved the sensation of his heart beating at a rapid rate.

Once he calmed down a little, he turned to look inside the glass.

Thankfully, there were no guards, so he took the chance to smash the window with his elbow. The second the window shattered, he crawled inside.

It appeared to be a bedroom, from the large, pink, floral designed bed to the right of him, and a huge cream colored dresser to the left of him.

It had wood flooring, and the wall paper was decorated with birds.

Around the window were many drawings hung on the walls. Some seemed to have been drawn by a child, but others were quite good.

They were all pictures of nature, such as trees, rivers, farmland and small creatures.

After Rumple was done looking around the room curiously, he remembered that he needed to get going.

When he approached the door, and tried to open it, he heard a high pitched voice pipe out "don't".

Rumple's head turned in the direction of the voice, and it seemed to be coming from the dresser.

"Hello? Is anyone there?" He asked, taking small steps closer to the dresser.

Hesitantly, the dresser door began to open, and a little girl stepped out.

She had long, black hair with bright green eyes and pale skin.

She whispered, "don't use the door."

Rumple stared at her in a baffled manner. "Who are you?" He asked.

She hesitated, then answered "My name is Snow... What's yours?"

"I-I'm Rumple." He replied.

She giggled, "Rumple? That's a funny name."

His head tilted, "really? I've always been told it's just a weird name, never funny."

The little girl shrugged, with a smile on her face. "Well," She said "If you want to get out of here, you can't use that door, an alarm with sound." She warned, "but, there is a secret door under the floor." She stated, pointing a few inches away from herself.

Rumple walked over to where she was pointing and knelt down.

"Is it under the wood?" He asked.

"No." She answered, "it's just magic."

"Magic?" Rumple questioned.

"Yes, my friend the fairy made it for me, so I can secretly wander the palace."

Snow knocked on the wood with a special beat, and a square shape formed in the wood, with a handle.

Snow lifted up the door and revealed a secret passageway.

It was a dark tunnel with a ladder built into it.

Rumple quickly grabbed onto the ladder and thanked the little girl.

With a sweet smile, the girl wished him farewell, and shut the door.

It was very dark in the tunnel, but Rumple managed to climb down.

When he reached the bottom, he saw an unlocked door.

Behind it was a room completely made out of cement and was not as pretty as the other rooms in the palace.

When Rumple looked to the left, he saw that the door leading out was a prison door.

This must have been the basement of the palace and also the prison.

Thankfully, the door wasn't locked and Rumple could get out.

He peered into the dark hallway outside of the cell. There were several more cell doors, but those were locked.

He heard creaking noises coming from down the hall, and he knew he wasn't alone.

With a bit of fear, he headed quickly towards the exit.

There were metal stairs heading up to the first floor of the palace, where a door to the outside would be available.

He climbed the stairs and found his escape.

With great speed, he sprinted into town.

He wasn't sure what to expect, since he's never been to a human town before.

When he walked through, many humans gave him strange looks, but he was too busy checking out the buildings that he didn't notice.

Wow... look how many stores!... He thought, gazing at the houses. When you looked around at the signs, he saw a pawn shop. *So that's what a pawn shop looks like...*

Where are the entryways to the tunnelments?... He wondered.

What is that?... He also wondered as he peered at a tomato.

A little boy ran up to Rumple, in a curious manner.

"Excuse me, mister." The little boy said.

"Oh, uh, yes?" Rumple responded.

"Why are you so short?" The little boy bluntly asked.

"Oh..." Rumple exhaled.

"Jack!" A woman yelled, jogging towards the little boy.

"What ma...?" Jack asked, not sure why his mother looked frustrated.

The woman looked at Rumple as though he was a criminal and dragged her son away.

Rumple could hear her scolding Jack as they walked away.

She said something on the lines of, "you never talk to strangers... especially ones that look like that."

When Rumple heard that, he felt a tension rise up inside of him. A feeling that he only felt when his mama would tell him not to go near the wall.

Rumple made his way through the town, and started to notice the looks.

He was much shorter than all of the humans, except for the children. With every human he crossed paths with, he was comparing to the first human he ever met.

Why are these humans so rude?... He wondered.

He peered up to the sky and saw that it was getting dark.

He needed a place to spend the night, but he wasn't sure where to go.

He knew that none of the humans were going to let him in, and he didn't even know where their tunnelments were.

Wherever he went, he would receive judgmental looks, and was always worried that they would try and attack him, like the Queen did.

When the night fell on the Kingdom, Rumple made his way to the stables and decided to sleep in the hay near the horses. The only beings that have been nice to him since he left his home.

Early that morning, Rumple went outside to find some food.

He searched around, but couldn't even find berries. So he figured he might find something to eat closer to the village.

There were barely any humans walking around that early in the morning, but he found a bush full of little blue berries, right next to what he perceived as a store.

He eagerly started to collect them, and since he was starving, he munched on some of them.

Right when he threw a second handful into his mouth, a lady came out of the building with a broom.

"Ahhh!" She yelled, as she swung the broom at Rumple's head.

"Get out!" She screamed, "Get off my property!"

Rumple hurriedly got up and ran off. He ran as far as he could. Far away from that village, far away from those humans.

He ran outside the Kingdom into the forest.

He remembered the Queen said that his home was about hundred miles outside of the Kingdom, through the forest, so that is where he headed.

It took him one and a half days of walking to get close to his home.

He barely slept, hardly ate anything; in fear something might be poisonous. The further he got into the abandoned forest, the more strange sounds he heard. He jumped and hid from shadows, and almost crept the entire way through. He heard the howling of beasts and threatening calls from other creatures.

Finally, he saw the wall, guarding his home.

He was so excited that he almost cried, but instead he ran towards it in joy.

"Help!" He cried, "help! I need a rope to climb!"

Another goblin peaked his head out from the top of the wall.

"Who goes there?!" He shouted.

"Me! I mean, Rumple! I'm one of you!" He shouted back.

"Rumple, eh?" The guard exclaimed, "You're the one that broke the law and climbed over the wall! We don't want you here!"

"What....?" Rumple muttered, "I thought that was just frowned upon... I didn't think it was illegal..."

"Well it is." The guard stated, with a nasty snare.

"Can I please come back?!" Rumple begged.

Before he could beg some more, the guard disappeared behind the wall.

"No!" Rumple screamed, "please! Let me back! Please! I'll never leave again! Please!" His pleading turned to sobs as he realized he was never going to be accepted back.

He sat pressed up against the wall for a few minutes, until he remembered the human who did this. Who talked him into giving up something precious in return for traveling this hideous world.

What a fool I am.... He thought, *I didn't even know what I was trading for....*

He was wandering the forest, trying to find shelter, when he stumbled upon the same river as last time.

He went to the edge and was surprised at how calm the water was, compared to last time.

He peered down at his reflection and noticed that he had a few scratches on his face.

All of the sudden, he heard strong rushing water coming his way.

Before he could get out, a wave of water crashed into him and swept him away.

An unknown amount of time passed, before Rumple awoke and found himself laid out on the river bed.

When he got up, he noticed a fallen tree across from him, that's branches dipped into the water.

Caught on those branches, was something that looked very familiar.

When he got closer, he finally remembered that it was the maroon hat that he bought from the old, human man.

He picked it up out of the water and decided to dry it.

He hung it up on a dried branch from another tree.

After a half an hour of waiting for the wind to take the water away, the hat was ready to wear.

When Rumple set the hat back on his head, the powerful feeling rushed back to him.

The feeling of being able to do anything.

Without even planning, Rumple with super speed built a log cabin where he stood. It was sturdy and he even was able to put in a fireplace.

After that, he made an oak tree grow apples, and a withered bush produce blueberries. When he touched the ground beneath him, the dirt turned into stone. He made a pathway from the river to his house and with a snap of his fingers he sparked a flame into his fireplace.

He could do anything, create anything, change anything. However, when he sat in the front of his cabin and stared out into the forest, he watched the birds in the air fly together. He watched the fish in the river swim together, and he watched even the wolves hunt together.

Oh how he wished he could be back with his own kind. The openness of the world was filled with many things, but it was so lonely.

Humans didn't want him, the animals were afraid of him and the goblins exiled him.

His family, his friends, his home... It wasn't just the feather he traded for this new life...

Am I the only one who has traded something too precious to lose?... He wondered.

When Rumple became bored at his cabin, he decided to go look for something new and interesting. Maybe another Kingdom.

As he traveled around, he got close to a village. He didn't want to get too close, knowing that humans were not friendly to goblins.

As he was passing the village, he saw a boy walking a cow outside of the village into the forest.

Rumple was very curious and followed the boy.

The boy and the cow walked for miles, until they stumbled upon an old man with a cart.

Rumple climbed a tree to see what was happening, and acknowledged that that was the same man who traded with him!

The old man talked to the boy for a moment, until the boy handed the cow over in exchange for a little brown bag.

The little boy ran off with the bag, and before the old man could get away, Rumple hopped down and shouted "hey! Stop!"

The old man turned around, and his lips broadened into a smile.

Rumple jogged up to him and yelled "what are you doing?! Are you going to ruin that boy's life like you did mine?!"

The old man looked at him in shock, "what do you mean?" He asked.

"I mean, I traded my life for this one!"

"And?..." The old man uttered.

Rumple's face became red with rage and he shouted "you ruined everything! I can't go back!"

"I thought you didn't want to go back?" The old man inquired.

"W-well I didn't understand what it would be like out here! It's horrible!"

The old man took a deep sigh and said "now you know you shouldn't make ignorant trades."

"What?..." Rumple muttered.

"You didn't understand what the outside world was like, but you traded what you did know for what you didn't!" The old man then pointed in the direction the little boy ran off to, "that boy didn't know what those beans do, but he traded his beloved cow for them! I've also made a deal with a beautiful woman who wanted to stay beautiful forever, so she traded her soul for it."

Rumple stared at him in awe.

As the old man tied the cow to the cart, he added "It's the desperate who make the blindest of trades."

With that, the old man strolled off into the forest, leaving Rumple there, alone.

Rumple traveled further, pondering what the old man had said. Then, he began to get hungry. So, he touched a willow tree and it produced ripe pears.

When he climbed to get one, he heard from behind him "wow! How did you do that!"

He looked behind himself and saw a middle aged man looking up in astonishment.

Rumple picked a pear then climbed down.

"It's magic." He replied.

"That's amazing!" The man exclaimed, "what else can you do?"

Rumple shrugged and answered "anything."

The man kicked the dirt beneath him and asked "if you can do anything... then can you help my village?"

Rumple looked at him curiously, "what's wrong with your village?"

The man answered "It's infested with rats. Nobody can get them out, but maybe you can!"

Rumple thought about this for a moment, and the man could see his hesitation. "I'll pay you! Fifty pounds!"

Rumple thought about it for another minute, then agreed.

He followed the man back to his village, then Rumple could tell the whole village was rat infested.

Grain was scattered all over the place and bags that once held food were ripped apart. Including the great amount of rat droppings in the street.

The man gathered his friends and neighbors around and announced "this is a man who can fix our rat problem! His name is!...." The man paused and looked at Rumple, asking with his eyes what his name was.

Then Rumple shouted to the crowd, "you can call me!... Rumpelstiltskin!"

The crowd cheered and Rumpelstiltskin formed a pipe in his hands. He stood on a bench in the street, and started playing a sweet tune.

All of the rats gathered around him, in a trance.

Then, with a ferocious note, the rats scattered and left the village behind.

The crowd cheered and began to chant. However, they couldn't pronounce the name Rumpelstiltskin, so they called him the Pied Piper.

After everyone celebrated, the man came up to Rumple with a sad expression on his face.

"What's the matter?" Rumple asked.

The man hesitated, then admitted "we don't have the money to pay you... Since the rats ate all of the grain, the village doesn't have much money left..."

Rumple glared at him, "you mean you lied to me?"

The man looked up from the ground, "I'm sorry... I was desperate is all... I didn't..."

Rumple threw the pipe to the ground and broke it, "desperate! Desperate enough to not trade at all!"

The man looked at Rumple in shock, "w-wh-wha–"

Rumple stormed off enraged.

He headed to the gate of the village, and when he reached it, he turned around and formed another pipe.

When he played the melody, all of the children in the village came running.

Then with another ferocious note, the children ran off into the forest.

"Pied Piper!" The villagers screamed, "what are you doing?!"

Before he left he turned back and growled, "my name is Rumpel-stiltskin."

Chapter Seven

Esther was a spoiled princess who got all she wanted. Her father, the King, was one of the richest Kings in the world, because he had unbelievable amounts of gold.

He had so much gold in fact, that the villagers believed that Esther's hair was a wig made of gold, because her hair was so blonde and shiny.

Esther's mother, Queen Sarah, would always make sure that whatever Esther asked for, Esther would get.

When they rode into town to wave to the commoners, Esther would always get a beautiful new dress and jewelry, but never say thank you in return.

Every store in the village knew how picky Esther could be, so they made sure when she came to town to have their best dresses on display.

Also, the restaurants knew to serve only the highest quality food and to make sure it was warm for their arrival.

Queen Sarah would also take Princess Esther jewelry shopping, and would only get the shiny gems, but not too shiny.

The pets in the pet stores were always groomed to perfection before Princess Esther touched them, so they would be soft, but not too soft.

The salons knew exactly what shampoos and conditioners to get for Princess Esther, because her hair was fragile.

One day, Esther decided she wanted to get a new pony.

Of course, the second she asked for it, the palace staff searched for the best pony in the Kingdom, and outside of the Kingdom.

After a few days, they found a white, good-looking pony to purchase.

They had never bothered testing the pony out before they bought it, they judged it on looks alone.

Once they got it looking as clean as could be, they sent Princess Esther down to have a look at it.

She gave her approval and wanted to ride it.

They tacked the pony up with the most comfortable, clean saddle and harness in the stable, and gave it to Esther.

When Esther hopped on and was being led to the arena ro ride, the pony freaked out and started running away, with Esther on his back!

The pony bolted into the village and galloped out of the Kingdom before the guards could reach her.

Esther held on to the pony as it galloped into the forest, except to get Esther off its back, he started bucking until she fell off.

She was too far away from the Kingdom's gate to know where she was.

She looked around but didn't see the village or even the wall surrounding the village.

She started screaming and crying for someone to hear her, but as she waited nobody came to her rescue.

She curled up against a willow tree, and began to sob.

As she sat there for hours, getting colder and colder and hungrier and hungrier, she smelled something in the distance.

It smelled good, so she followed the scent.

It led her a mile further into the woods, but she eventually stumbled upon a cute cottage.

It had smoke coming out of the chimney, and looked warm.

She wanted inside, so she knocked on the door.

"Hello?" She exclaimed, "hello?" She said again as she knocked on the door.

Nobody answered, so she figured nobody was home.

She wanted to get inside so badly, so she tested the door knob.

When she turned it, the door creaked open.

She peered inside and didn't see anybody, so she walked in.

Inside she got a big whiff of what she had been smelling. Three bowls of porridge were sitting on a table, and when Esther saw them, her stomach growled.

So, she tasted the big bowl of porridge, but it was too hot. Then, she tasted the medium sized bowl, but it was too cold. Lastly, she tasted the small bowl, and it was neither too hot nor too cold, but just right. So she gobbled all of it up.

Once her belly was full, she noticed how tired her feet were from walking, so she decided to sit in one of the chairs.

The big chair was too hard for her, but the medium-sized chair was too soft for her. Lastly, she tried the small chair, and it was just right. However, once she made herself comfortable in it, the legs broke!

She fell on her butt, and decided she was too tired from today.

So, she headed upstairs and into the bedroom. She saw three beds and tested the big one first, but the head was too tall for her. Then, she tested the medium-sized one, but that was too high at the foot for her, so she lastly tried the small bed, and it was just right.

Without any regard for the home owners, she fell asleep in the little bed.

After a long time, she felt a tap on her shoulder and heard a low growl.

When she looked up, she saw three bears standing over her.

She screamed with terror and ran out of the room.

The bears chased her, in anger, deeper into the woods.

She screamed the entire time she ran, until they finally let her go.

It was dark out, and she heard noises all around her.

"Ah!" She shouted when she heard a twig snap.

"Eh!" She squealed when she heard the flapping of a bird's wings.

Again, she started to sob.

"I just want to go home!" She cried.

Just then, someone appeared to her. She screamed when she saw his shadow, but when he stepped into light she saw he was her size.

"W-Who are you?" She asked with fear.

"My name doesn't matter darling, who are you?"

He wore a maroon hat and tattered green pants and shirt.

"I-I'm Esther..." She replied.

"Esther?..." The little man muttered.

"M-mhm." She responded.

The little man grinned, "you don't happen to be Princess Esther, are you?"

"Uh, yes, I am."

His grin grew bigger, "oh, well in that case, my name is Rumpel-stiltskin, but you can call me Rumple."

He shook her hand, then added "I know a warm place you can sleep."

"Really?" Esther asked with excitement.

"Of course!" Rumple exclaimed, "follow me!"

Esther followed Rumple a long ways into the forest, until she heard rushing water.

When they got closer, she also saw a cabin.

When Rumple snapped his fingers, the cabin's lights went on.

They entered the cabin and it was larger on the inside than it appeared on the inside.

The kitchen was to the right and the living space was in the middle. Behind the sofas were two doors.

Rumple pointed at the door on the left, "that will be your room." He stated.

When Esther looked inside, it was a decent sized room with a window to the left and a closet to the right.

"Is there a bed?" She asked.

Rumple chuckled, "of course, my dear."

Then, a bed appeared in the middle of the room. It had pink covers and two fluffy pillows.

"Wow! How did you do that?!" She asked in astonishment.

"It's called magic." He replied.

"Thank you so much." Esther exclaimed.

With another grin, Rumple responded "of course."

Esther believed that she would spend one night, then he would take her back home.

However, she spent the day and the next night there too. She really didn't mind, because whatever she asked for, Rumple would provide.

She asked for a new outfit that she could wear that day, and within seconds she would have a gorgeous new dress.

He spoiled her with goods and magic tricks that kept her attention, till she was there for days and didn't even notice. Nights passed, but for her it seemed like hours. Before she knew it, she had two closets full of clothes, a room flooded with toys and accessories, along with a backyard garden that could grow anything she could think up.

Every once in a while, Rumple would take Esther out for walks, to go wander the forest. One day, they heard shouting in the forest.

Rumple seemed alarmed by the men's shouts in the distance, and hurried Esther away from them.

When they got back to the cabin, Esther asked "what was that yelling? Why did we leave so fast?"

Rumple hesitated to answer, but eventually made up the excuse, "in these woods, there are coyotes that attract human prey by sounding like humans themselves. I just didn't want us getting hurt..."

Esther nodded, then headed to her room.

She gazed out her window at the vast forest that surrounded her.

Then, she looked at the toys and clothes that Rumple gifted her, that shimmered around the, now, recognizably small room.

At that moment, she realized, *wow, what am I still doing here?*

She decided to go confront Rumple, who was sitting in the living room reading a book.

"Rumple..." Esther began.

"Yes, princess?" Rumple replied.

"...I was wondering why I'm still here... Are you going to bring me back home soon?"

Rumple closed his book with a scornful look.

"What do you mean?" He asked, trying to sound fine even though he obviously wasn't.

Esther glanced over at the door, then back to Rumple, "It's just... It's just... I know my parents are probably looking for me... And I... And I..."

Esther felt the glare prickling her skin and a sense of fear rush over her. The cabin felt like it was shrinking and the harsh glare got closer and closer.

"I-I...I'm gonna go back to my room now!" Esther squealed, then darted back into her room, closing the door behind her.

She took a few sharp breaths, then a few very deep breaths to calm herself down.

After a little while of laying on her bed, she inched closer to the window. She looked out, but it was already dark.

Where are those voices now?...

Years passed and Esther grew up. She could tell from the mirror that she grew and her face matured over every year. Her gold hair grew down to her waist and her once round face started to show cheek bones.

One day, Esther heard a knock on the door. It had been the first knock she had heard in 4 years, so she looked outside her window.

From her bedroom, she heard Rumple open the door and a slight mumble come through the wall.

The man outside the cabin was tall and handsome, with dark hair and what looked like dark eyes to match.

Rumple closed the door and Esther heard rustling in the cabin.

As Esther peered out the window, the man spotted her staring. However, the second he saw her, Rumple re-opened the door and caught his attention.

As he was discussing with Rumple, Esther ducked back into her room. She slid the curtain over her window and picked up a book.

The story she was reading about was a true story that had happened 100 years ago, to a kidnapped princess.

The princess was born with beautiful, long hair, but when she was a baby she was taken by an evil woman. The evil woman imprisoned her in a tall tower, until she escaped with the help of a prince who climbed the tower using her long hair.

Esther pressed the book against her chest and let out a deep sigh.

How unfortunate that there is no prince here to save me... She thought.

She ran her fingers through her hair and gazed up at the ceiling.

Maybe I can grow my hair out longer and create a rope to lead a prince here...

A few more days passed by and Esther spent her days reading more romance novels.

So many stories have different meanings, beginnings and ends, however they all revolved around finding true love.

For some reason, Esther had seemed obsessed with that plot recently.

Rumple peaked his head into her room through the door and asked "would you like to go for a walk?"

"Yeah..." She replied, while she got up from the bed.

The air that afternoon was brisk, and Esther could feel that there would be a storm coming soon. Being trapped in a room and having no distractions from the outside world, you learn the silent secrets of nature.

They passed by the same willow tree that they do every time, but there was a new mark slashed onto the bark.

It could have been an animals' claw, but it was a singular, clean slash.

Esther thought of mentioning it, but decided to keep her mouth shut.

Further into the forest, down the usual path–that Esther could walk through blindfolded– they made it to the Oval Oak Tree; an oak tree that's trunk was 6 yards wide and in the shape of an oval.

Before they were ready to head back to the cabin, they heard hacking sounds not too far away from them.

Esther recognized the sound and identified it with the noise a sword makes against a tree.

Rumple grabbed her arm, concerningly dragging her back.

Esther allowed him to pull her away and even lie to her when they arrived back at the cabin.

"I'm sorry, Esther, but I couldn't waste any time. That clanging sound we heard was of a beast. It's rare to come into contact with them, but their claws against a tree make that noise. I couldn't let you get any closer, in fear that it might attack."

He tried to sound as sincere as possible, through his lying lips, but Esther knew better.

That night, Esther couldn't get a wink of sleep.

She peered outside her window into the darkness, hoping to see another human.

Her eyes strained to make out the dark figures in the woods, but all she could see were the trees.

When midnight struck, Esther knew Rumple would be asleep.

Stealthily, she tip-toed across the wooden floors to the door.

She slowly twisted the knob and creaked it open. The hinges produced a high-pitched squeak, and Esther's stomach dropped. Her muscles froze in an uncomfortable position, and she waited a few minutes–dreading every second– until she realized he wasn't coming to check out the suspicious sound.

She proceeded to inch her way out of the cabin, continuing to tip-toe even when she was outside.

The darkness didn't decimate her ability to navigate through the woods, due to her experience on their walks.

She went down the known path and eventually made it to the willow tree. She examined the slash mark on the trunk and established to herself that it definitely was not a claw mark.

She pursued down the path and when she got to the Oval Oak Tree she looked around.

She listened for the clanging noises, or footsteps, but didn't hear anything except for the owls and the shaking of the leaves.

For hours, she searched around the area and finally found the tree that got chipped away by a sword. They were the same slashes she saw on the willow tree.

Around the trunk of the tree were footprints in the mud.

They were not her footprints, because these were much larger than hers.

They were human and were headed in a different direction than she came from.

She followed the footprints that eventually led her to an orange glow in the distance.

As she got closer, an image came into view. It was of a man sitting on a stump, warming his hands up against the heat of a fire.

Esther was so startled by seeing a human for the first time in 3 years, that she hid behind a tree. Then she acknowledged that this man wasn't necessarily a good man either. She didn't know him and had no clue at where he came from.

He could be from a dark kingdom... She thought.

She stayed there till morning, worried that if she went back, she would be caught by Rumple and never be let outside again.

In the morning, the man put out the fire and packed up his belongings.

While he did so, he hummed a sweet tune.

Esther believed, a man who sings a kind tune must be kind himself...

She watched him walk away and followed him. She kept her distance and made sure he didn't know she was following him.

She stalked him for hours, crossing rivers and swamps as she did so.

He would take short breaks between hours of traveling, and sit down and maybe eat something.

Watching him eat made Esther incredibly hungry, almost to the point where she wanted to show herself, just to get a bite to eat.

But she controlled herself, knowing that a decision like that could mean life or death.

She followed him for several more hours, and during that time they crossed an open field.

She ducked down into the tall weeds so she wouldn't be noticed, and took that opportunity to munch on some flowers as she crawled through.

When she got up out of the field, her hands and knees felt prickly and her hair was knotted and felt as though bigs were swarming her scalp.

However, she continued to follow the man.

They spent another night in the forest, and Esther climbed a tree so she wouldn't get attacked by a predator.

She looked the man over, and acknowledged that he was quite handsome.

He looked young and had thick, dark hair, that probably with a shower would become smooth and shiny.

She couldn't sleep due to the uncomfortable branch she was laying on, but he seemed to sleep just fine.

Early in the morning, he got up and swiftly packed up his belongings.

After another day of traveling, they reached an ocean.

An ocean that Esther had never seen before.

Waiting for the man on the end of the dock was a little wooden boat with an expecting looking man.

They waved at each other and the man hopped into the boat.

The other man began to row away from the dock, further out into the ocean.

Esther looked behind her, but had no idea where she was or how to get back to the cabin—not that she wanted to go back—.

She scouted to find another boat or something to float on, but didn't see anything on the beach.

When she almost gave up hope, she noticed, what looked like, a piece of wood from the corner of her eye, tucked inside the bushes in the forest.

She pulled it out and saw that it was a wooden raft. She didn't find any paddles to row with, but she did rip a plank off the dock to use it as a paddle.

She eventually got the hang of propelling the raft, and paddled as fast as she could to catch up with them. However, she lost them in the distance.

She looked around frantically to find land or another boat, but none was in sight.

She rowed forward, in hopes of eventually finding land, but her arms grew tired and the starving pain got to her.

She laid down on the raft underneath the scorching sun. There were no clouds in the sky to shield her from the direct heat and she could feel the skin on her face becoming dry and hot.

After a few more hours went by, the sun retreated into the horizon and the sky went dark.

Her whole mouth and throat were parched and her stomach was still eating itself.

She drifted with the direction of the wind and at last, land came into sight. Esther used all the strength she had left to maneuver her way to shore. She dragged it onto the sand and when she looked up the hill she saw a castle.

This is a kingdom.... She acknowledged.

She stumbled her way to the stairs leading up the hill. She climbed up them on her hands and knees, and rested for a while when she reached the top.

When she gained a little more strength to head to the castle, she went up to the castle gate. In order to get past the guards, she got a black blanket to hide in the shadows.

She was able to sneak around them and get to a door.

This castle was significantly smaller than the one she grew up in, but it had to still belong to a King and Queen.

She knocked on the door and luckily someone opened it. It was a servant, but Esther quickly exclaimed "I'm a princess."

The servant looked at her skeptically, but an elderly woman dressed in a purple nightgown came up behind her.

"Did you just say you are a princess?" The woman asked.

Esther nodded desperately.

The woman looked behind her then back at Esther, "come in, come in."

She told Esther.

Esther was led into the grand foyer of the castle, and was welcomed by an elderly man wearing a purple robe.

They both stood before her and introduced themselves, "hello," the woman greeted "I am Queen Debra, and this is my husband, King Nathaniel."

Esther curtsied in front of them, but the Queen still looked skeptical.

She gestured for Esther to follow her, so she did.

Two female servants tagged along and they ended up in a large bedroom.

It had bright yellow walls and a single bed in the center of the room.

The Queen turned to face Esther and asked "do you mind if I test you to make sure you are a princess? Just to make sure I'm not being fooled here."

Esther agreed, knowing she would pass because she truly was a princess.

The Queen snapped her fingers at the two servants and they quickly ran out of the room. A few moments later multiple servants came in, each dragging a mattress with them. They piled them up on top of the single mattress already on the bed frame, until there were 20 mattresses stacked together.

"This is where you will be sleeping. Does it look suitable for you?"

Esther looked it up and down, then compared this obvious test with the princess' posture test; where they stack books on top of the princess' head to see if she could balance them.

"Yes, this looks lovely." Esther replied, accepting the challenge.

She climbed up the bed and made it to the top.

During the night, she kept feeling a lump in the mattress. Something wasn't perfect, and it kept her up all night.

In the morning, a servant called her to the dining room for breakfast.

She climbed down and was led into the dining room where the King, Queen and a familiar looking man were already sitting down.

When Esther sat down, the Queen asked "How did you sleep, Esther?"

Esther looked down at her plate, embarrassed, believing she failed the test, but she answered truthfully, "I didn't sleep well at all ... .There was a constant pain in my back."

The Queen's lips broadend into a wide grin. "You are a princess!" She exclaimed joyfully.

She immediately stood up and went over to her son, setting her hands on his shoulders.

"This is Prince Damian! And he has traveled the world in search of a princess, but instead one found him!" She expressed.

Prince Damian stood up and made his way over to Esther.

Esther stood up too when he approached her, and he kissed her hand.

"Princess....?" He inquired.

"Esther... Princess Esther."

"What a lovely name."

"Thank you."

About the author

***

Lauren Anderson is a teenager from Grand Rapids, Michigan.

Her love of storytelling is much greater than her love of writing,

but she still dreams and works hard at becoming an author of many more books of different genres. Along with, hopefully, having the opportunity to produce a movie one day.

She hasn't graduated high school, yet, but she will continue to publish books during her high school career, as well as making it her career in the future.

Lauren wrote The Unknown Tales because she has grown up loving fairy tales and thought it would be a great and fun idea to tell the stories of the characters no one may have heard before.

This book is only the first of many for Lauren Anderson and she can't wait to publish again.

www.ingramcontent.com/pod-product-compliance
Lightning Source LLC
Chambersburg PA
CBHW050318110726
47899CB00007B/2292